CITADEL OF THE STAR LORDS

By
EDMOND HAMILTON

I0616774

ARMCHAIR FICTION
PO Box 4369, Medford, Oregon 97504

For more information about Armchair Books and products, visit our website at…

www.armchairfiction.com

Or email us at…

armchairfiction@yahoo.com

THE EARTH UNDER ALIEN RULE!

One moment Price was on the run, in his small plane, being pursued by a squad of military jets. Then suddenly the jets veered off and Price thought he had somehow eluded them. He was safe. However, a moment later the whole sky lit up in a blinding light and he was flung far, far into the future, into a world where mankind no longer ruled their own planet. The entire human race had been reduced to rubble, living in a world where marauding alien hordes ruled the surface of the Earth.

The scattered remains of humanity cried out bitterly for revenge and they turned to Price, a man from the past, for help. But what was the true alien horror that threatened total annihilation, and could it be stopped?

FOR A COMPLETE SECOND NOVEL, TURN TO PAGE 85

CAST OF CHARACTERS

PRICE
He just wanted to get away from the cops. But he ended up nearly a hundred years into the future on a shattered Earth.

LINNA OF VRAIN FOUR
She was a beautiful woman from another world, part of the alien force that now kept the remnants of humanity at bay.

ARRIN
As the leader of the aliens that now ruled the Earth, he gave mankind a choice: hand over Price—or be destroyed!

SAWYER
The wise, yet bitter leader of the Missouris. No one wanted revenge against the Vurna more than he did.

TWIST
A wily hunter and a respected warrior, he was the first to realize the importance of this strange man from the past.

BURR
Another fierce warrior of the future. All he wanted to do was cut Price's throat!

CHAPTER ONE

AS HE GUNNED his plane northward through the night, Price thought of the roller coaster when he'd been a kid, of how you went faster and faster until you hit the big plunge.

Well, he was on the big plunge now. And what would end this roller-coaster ride—prison, or escape, or a crash? It had to be one of those.

He was to remember that, later. He was to think later that it was well he didn't dream the fantastic fate he was really racing toward…

He looked down, and there was only blackness. The deserts of California and Nevada are dark and wide, and he was keeping well away from the airways beacons and the main highways.

He kept the Beechcraft as high as he could. He was flying without lights, but with what they already had against him, that minor infraction wasn't important. He kept looking back, expecting every minute to see the red-and-green wing-lights of Border Patrol planes coming up on his tail.

If he was lucky, if he slipped them long enough, if he crossed north without being sighted by the passenger planes that shuttled between Las Vegas and Los Angeles, he might just make it to Bill Willerman's and get the Beechcraft under cover. If—if—if—

There was another if, Price thought bitterly. If he'd had any brains, he wouldn't be in this spot at all.

He turned on the radio. He flipped the dial around, getting loud music from a Vegas hotel, then a political speech, then more music—and then a news broadcast. As he'd expected, he was at the top of the news.

"...so that even while Arnolfo Ruiz, firebrand revolutionary exile, is under arrest by Mexican police, United States authorities are conducting an intensive air dragnet search for the American pilot who smuggled Ruiz across the border. That unknown pilot is known to have returned across

CITADEL OF THE STAR LORDS
by
Edmond Hamilton

Out of the dark vastness of the void came a conquering horde, incredible and invincible, with Earth's only weapon — a man from the past!

the border an hour ago, and police of three states have been alerted.

"The AEC announces that its next test will be that of an experimental small new H-bomb whose effects will be studied for..."

Price savagely cut the radio. He damned the announcer, and Ruiz, and himself. Most of all, himself.

He'd acted like a halfwit. Because a smooth talker had given him a phony story about a secret business trip, he had smuggled the most dangerous troublemaker in the hemisphere down into a friendly republic. Who would believe he hadn't known? He had done it, and pressure from Washington would make sure that he got full pay for his folly.

He might as well look the truth in the face. If it hadn't been this, it would have been something else. He'd been playing the fool for years, ever since Korea. Other fliers had come home from there and taken up their jobs again, but a job had been too dull for him; he'd drifted along with the fast buck fly-boys out for fun and excitement, hauling hunting and fishing parties, spending the profits in bordertown bars, going broke and starting over again—and now finally this. His roller coaster ride was about over.

It would be over for good if he didn't reach Willerman's ranch before daylight. Bill would hide the plane for him. He'd saved Bill's neck a couple of times in the old days, and he could depend on him. But he had to reach him, first.

He saw the glow in the sky that came from the lights of Las Vegas, and he kept warily wide of it. He looked back again. No Patrol planes yet. As he rushed on, Price began to feel that he was going to make it.

Then, suddenly and disastrously, everything happened at once.

He saw lights on the ground ahead—an oddly scattered pattern of lights too thin to be a town, too widespread to be a ranch.

At the same moment, two fast jets screamed down from the upper darkness and nearly tore his wings off. They curved around for another pass at him.

"Air Force planes!" thought Price. "Hell, that tears it…"

It seemed crazy that the government was that hot to catch him. But the jets were making another lightning pass to him, trying to scare him, to force him down.

He had less than a chance in a million to lose them, and he knew it. But he was going to be a long time in jail, and he might as well give them a run for it. Just possibly, the slower Beechcraft could get away in the dark the next time they overshot him.

He gunned the plane wide open, rushing high over the scattered lights. And then, incredibly, he was free of his pursuers. He looked over his shoulder and saw them drawing back.

It didn't make sense. Why would they suddenly draw back? Anyway, with those jets off his tail, he still had a chance.

Price looked down. Among the lights down there he saw lights on a queer steel tower. He'd seen pictures of a tower like that somewhere. It wasn't an oilrig, but something he couldn't remember.

And then, suddenly, he remembered, and a terrible coldness choked him and his flesh flinched as he saw a door into nightmare opening.

That tower, and the announcement of a new H-bomb test, and the distance he was from Vegas, and the way those frantic jets had drawn back...

"Oh, no," said Price. "Oh, no, oh no, oh no—"

He was still saying it when the bomb went off and the universe cracked wide open under his racing plane.

CHAPTER TWO

THE CATACLYSM that hit Price was without light or sound. That, when he thought of it later, was the most awful feature of it.

He felt a shock, but not the shock of ultimate annihilation he expected. This was a shuddering impact as of the plane, himself, hitting some barrier and forcing through, a rending, tearing, dizzying thing that was like no sensation he had ever experienced.

He yelled, naked terror forcing the air from his lungs. His weight flung against the straps, and he knew from that that the plane was in a spin. Mechanically, his hands reached to the controls. He leveled off...

But he wasn't dead. He was alive, undestroyed, and how could that be if the raving energies of a hydrogen bomb had been unloosed beneath him?

Price's mind was a mad turmoil. What had happened?

He had blundered right over the bomb test-area, right over the bomb-tower. And the jets guarding the area had tried to stop him. Probably, if his radio hadn't been off, he would have heard them screaming frantic warnings to him.

But had the bomb really gone off? If it had, he would surely have been instantly annihilated.

He hadn't been. He was alive. The plane was ticking along through the night. The instruments functioned.

But *something* terrific had happened. That ghastly, wrenching shock that had seemed to outrage the very atoms of his body—his flesh still crawled with the memory of it. Something had happened. But what?

Price couldn't think. The mind just could not grapple with

a thing like this. He sat, mechanically touching the controls, and the Beechcraft roared on and on.

Gradually, his mind came alive. He shakily swung the plane around. He was going back to Las Vegas. Right now, arrest and prison looked good to him compared to what had happened, or nearly happened.

If he hadn't been so tensely trying to escape, he thought, he would have remembered about the bomb-tests coming up. There had been newspaper stories. Guarded stories about a radical physical effect detected during explosions of the new-type H-bombs, and mention of elaborate preparations being made to study these unusual effects.

Price's thoughts leaped suddenly. He recalled a scientist's statement that the center of explosion of the new-type bomb might be like the eye of a hurricane, a focus of inconceivable forces but affected in a radically different way by those forces.

Had the bomb gone off under him, then? Had his plane and himself, at the "eye" of the tremendous explosion, been hurled somehow through spatial barriers into safety before the light and sound and destruction could even reach him?

It seemed an insane speculation. Yet everything about this was insane. He would be himself, if he didn't get down to Earth soon.

He could not see the glow of Las Vegas anywhere in the night. He cut his radio in and spoke hoarsely into it.

"Beechcraft 4556 calling Las Vegas Airport! Come in, Las Vegas!"

There was no answer. The radio seemed operative, but when he turned the receiver dials, not a sound came out.

"Knocked out," Price muttered. "And no wonder, if…"

He couldn't finish the thought, it was too soul-shaking a thing to speculate on, the thing that might have happened to him.

He curved the plane around, looking for highway lights,

for an airway beacon, anything.

Nothing. Nothing but the darkness and the stars.

A LITTLE frantically, he swung the plane around and started eastward again. He must have missed Las Vegas. But if he kept going east, he'd surely cut the main highways. There were always lots of cars on them at night, in the summer.

He flew on and on. And the darkness continued. No lights at all, not even the glimmer from a lonely ranch.

Nothing.

He would have landed, gladly now, but he did not know where he was or what was under him. The Beechcraft was equipped with extra fuel tanks for long flights away from any source of supply, and they had been full when he started. He could fly a long time yet.

He flew.

After a while he began to think that there was only one explanation. He was dead, and flying in limbo. And limbo, it seemed, went on forever.

Finally, after many hours there began to be a light in the blackness ahead of him, and his heart leaped up, thinking that at last he had raised the glow of a big town. But it was only the dawn. He watched it creep cold and gray across the world, and now he understood that he was alive. But he was not cheered. Now he could see what was underneath him.

Forest. Rolling like a dark green sea from north to south, from east to west. He had left the desert far behind. He figured that he was over Missouri now, and there should have been towns, villages, farms, cultivated fields.

There was forest.

The light turned rosy, then golden. The sun sprang up and it was day. Far ahead the Mississippi gleamed. Price sent the Beechcraft at full throttle, toward St. Louis. He could not see any smoke from the great complex of city and industry that sprawled there over both banks of the river, and he could not see any bridges. But St. Louis had to be there.

It was. But it had changed since he saw it last. The high buildings were brought low, and the low buildings were mounds, shells covered with brush and foxgrape, and trees grew in the public streets and through the broken windows. The river, vast and placid, was empty except for a floating log. Obstructions along the shores might once have been docks, but were so no longer. And there was a great stillness.

For one wild moment Price thought. The *bomb did it last night, the new-type bomb with energies they didn't even dream about.* Then he realized that that was hardly possible. You can destroy a city with an H-bomb in a matter of seconds, but you can't grow an oak tree sixty feet high in the rubble of the City Hall in much under a century.

Time had passed since last night.

This was too much to take in all at once. Price didn't even try. He looked for a place to land, but there wasn't any, so he kept on flying, eastward across the river.

Time had passed, and he had passed with it. Slowly it began to come to Price, the dreadful and incredible truth of what had happened. The wrenching, tearing shock he had felt in the eye of the blast was not physical but temporal. The uncomprehended powers of the bomb had been mightier than anyone had guessed. They warped the ordered fabric of the space-time continuum itself, and acting on the matter of himself and his plane at the "eye" of the explosion, had warped them too—into the future.

The Beechcraft went droning through the empty sky. Price looked down on desolation, green and peaceful and as unproductive as it had been before men ever came with axe and plow to tame it.

How far in the future?

He did not know.

Were there still men, surviving somewhere in this wilderness? Or had humanity destroyed itself in a final act of atomic madness? Were all the cities dead and dust?

He did not know that either.

He only knew that he was too numb and exhausted to go much farther. He had to have water and food and sleep. He had to have a place to land.

HE FOUND IT well beyond the river, a natural prairie in the midst of trees. He tried to gauge the way the wind was blowing by the ripple of the grass, and then he circled in a long curve to the north to head it. As he did so he thought he saw an iron glinting to the northeast, something very vast and strange as of the sun reflecting from a face of metal mountain-high and wide. Then he dropped low over the treetops, and whatever the glinting was he could not see it any more.

The Beechcraft bumped and bounded to a stop. Price sat for a moment watching his hands shake on the controls, and then some last measure of caution made him taxi the plane back to the extreme edge of the prairie and nose it into the wind, ready to take off again with no delay.

He had a sporting rifle and revolver in the plane. He buckled on the revolver, stuffed his pockets full of cartridges for the rifle, and climbed down to the ground. He stood for several minutes in the shelter of the plane's wing, looking around, but he could not see any signs of life except a pair of crows flapping over his head with rusty cawing. It was late summer, and the wind was dry and hot. He began to walk toward the woods.

He looked a little dazedly, as he walked, toward the northeast. What was it, the incredible iron vastness he had glimpsed far away there?

About thirty yards from the plane Price stopped suddenly, his heart pounding and a sudden sweat breaking on his skin. The grass was trampled here in an irregular circle, with scars of bare earth ripped in the ground. There was a large quantity of blood, scarcely dry. A wide flattened track led to the woods. Something had been killed here, something big, like a horse or a cow, and the carcass dragged in among the trees.

Men. Hunters. An animal would have devoured its kill where it lay.

But what kind of men?

Price stood half-crouched over the bloody ground, his rifle ready, looking this way and that and seeing nothing. The hot wind went running over the prairie and the encircling trees bowed to it and tossed their branches, but there was no other motion, no other sound. Even the crows had gone.

Price shouted. "Hello! Hello! Is anybody there? I'm lost. I need help. Hello!"

His voice was shocking in the stillness, loud and impolite.

There was no answer.

He went on down the flattened track toward the trees. He was afraid, and desperately tired.

"Hello?" he said, and now his voice was pleading. "Please. Where are you? Help me—"

Help me, you men of an unknown future, you Hunters in impossibility, you lurkers in nightmare. Help me, or I die.

The shadows were heavy under the trees. The prairie grass did not grow here, but there were briars and other things to show a crushed trail. It was not a long one. He saw the carcass lying in a little glade. It was a black and white cow, already partially butchered. He moved toward it, and then from the branches overhead and the underbrush on either side short ropes of braided leather came flying, weighted at their ends with stones. Price fell down helpless and floundering, painfully bruised, his arms and legs wrapped in the tough bolo-like ropes, and one around his neck cutting off his breath so he could not even cry out.

In a swift and furious rush six men sprang from among the trees and stood menacingly about him. One of them snatched his rifle, while another grabbed his revolver. They wore sketchy old garments of tanned leather, and they were as dark and wild as the Shawnees and Wyandots who had hunted these woodland prairies long ago, except that some of them had light hair and all of them were bearded.

One of them, a tall lean wide-shouldered man with a shock of sun-bleached brown hair and eyes more blue, more blazing and filled with hate than any Price could remember seeing in his life, crouched beside him and tore the strangling rope urgently from his neck. Price tried to speak, but before he could do more than gasp for breath the brown-haired man whipped out a knife and drove the point of it straight for Price's throat.

"Now," he said, "you starspawn—we'll see if your blood is any redder than the kind we breed on Earth!"

The steel bit hard. Price screamed.

CHAPTER THREE

THE BROWN-HAIRED man withdrew the knife with a nice dexterity, its tip reddened for perhaps a quarter of an inch. Price looked at it and at him in dumb horror. The six wolfish faces collected in a close circle above him and peered down, smiling.

"It's the same color, Burr. Who'd have thought it?"

"Just blood. Hah! And I always thought they'd bleed hard and shiny, like quicksilver."

"Stick him again, Burr."

"I wish we had time," said Burr, and licked his lips with a red tongue. "But they know where we are." He sighed and raised the knife again. "We got to get out of here. Fast."

Price found his voice. "For God's sake," he cried. "For God's sake, what are you doing? I ask you for help, and you..." He struggled furiously against the ropes. "You haven't any right to kill me. I haven't done you any harm."

"Star-spawn," said Burr softly, using that word for the second time. He prodded Price above the belt with the knifepoint. "If I had time I'd do this slowly, very slowly. Be glad we don't have time."

"But why?" Price shouted. "What for?" He glared up at the circle of hairy faces. "I only got here today. I couldn't have done anything to you. I came from..."

From yesterday? A hundred years ago? Through time? Tell them, and ask them to believe it. Maybe they will. I don't.

"...from the West," he said. "From Nevada. I haven't anything to do with stars."

Burr laughed. He raised the knife. But another man, with a shrewd dark eye and gray hairs in his beard, caught his wrist.

"Wait a minute. Look at his hair. It's as dark as mine."

"Dyed," said Burr. "Look at his clothes. Look at the flier he came in, at his weapons. Look where he is…in the Forbidden Belt. If he isn't from the Citadel …don't be a foolish man, Twist. Let go."

"Why would he dye his hair to look like a human and then come to us in a flier? Is that reasonable? Now hold on, Burr. You hear me? There's a way to tell."

Burr grumbled, but he relaxed, and Twist let him go. He caught Price by the collar and dragged him into the glade by the butchered cow, where the sunlight fell in strong shafts. Then he rolled Price's head back and forth, studying it with intense interest. The others looked over his shoulder.

"His eyes are dark too," said Twist. "You can't dye eyeballs. And look here. See that, Burr? Feel it. He's got the sproutings of a beard. Now we all know the Star Lords don't grow hair on their lovely faces."

"Hey," said the others. "That's right. Twist is right."

"Of course he's right," said Price. "I'm human." He knew that much. The rest of the talk was a mystery, but that didn't matter. Not right now. "I come from the West. I'm a friend."

Burr looked sullen. "Humans don't fly. Only Star Lords do that."

"Maybe he's a collaborator?" said a yellow-haired boy, all bright and eager, and Burr smiled again.

"Maybe. Anyway, he's none of us. Stand by, Twist."

But Twist did not stand by. He faced the others in fatherly anger at their stupidity.

"You're almighty anxious for a killing Burr. Now what's the Chief going to say when we come back and tell him that a human man came in an airplane, and asked us for help, and we stuck him like a pig and left the plane for the Star Lords?"

For some reason the word "plane" sobered them down and made them thoughtful. Twist pressed his advantage.

"You've all seen the old pictures. You know this flier isn't from the Citadel. It ain't the same shape and it don't make the same noise. It's a plane. Maybe the last one on Earth, and this man knows how to fly it. And you want to cut his throat?"

There was a short silence, during which Price thought he could hear the drops of sweat trickling down his forehead. Then Burr said, without rancor,

"I guess you're right. We'd better take him to the Chief."

"All right," said Twist. He crouched down and began unwrapping the bolo ropes. Price said, "Thanks." It seemed a very small word, and inadequate. Twist grunted.

"If you prove out to be a collaborator," he said, "you'll wish I'd let you die an easy death."

"I'm not," said Price. His brain had been working with abnormal speed. "This is an—an *old* plane. The papers are still in it. It's been kept hidden, except—" He groped desperately for explanations. "It's a tradition in my family to fly. We're taught, father to son."

That was true enough. Price's father had taken to the air in World War I, and for years afterward had run a flying service. The rest of it he had to play by ear, and God help him if he guessed wrong.

TWIST HELPED him to his feet. "Now," he said to the others, "I want to know what about that plane."

"Get it under cover," Burr said. "Hide it."

"We might do that," Twist said. "And the first flying-eye that happened along would find it. They do more than see, you know. They smell, too. They smell metal, if it's much bigger than a knife." He held out the stone-weighted ropes and shook them. "That's why we use these when we hunt in the Belt. Remember?"

"Now, there's no call to be jeering, Twist," said Burr. "If you got a better idea, we'll listen to it."

"Fly it out," said Twist sharply. "How else are we going to get it to the Chief? On our backs? Cut up and packed on the horses? No." He turned to the man who had taken Price's pistol. "Give me that, Larkin. And you, Harper, hand that rifle to Burr. Larkin, you're in charge of the party. Get the beef back to the camp, and as soon as you've smoked it load up and head home. Keep an eye out for trouble...this is liable to poke up the Citadel like you'd poke a beehive."

Larkin, a short powerful man with a curly poll like a certain type of bull Price had once seen, asked in a mild high voice, "Where are you and Burr going?"

Twist pointed a thumb skyward. "Up there," he said, and his eyes shone with excitement. He looked at Burr and grinned.

Burr was scared. It showed in his eyes, in the way his mouth tightened. But he wouldn't say so. Instead he reached out and grabbed Price by the shirt and shook him fiercely.

"There'll be a gun at your head every minute, and don't you forget. You do anything wrong, and you're dead."

Price forbore to explain what would happen to Burr and Twist if they shot him in mid-air. He only nodded and said,

"Don't worry. I'm as anxious to get to your Chief as you are." He took a deep breath and plunged. "That's what I came for."

Burr said, "You're a long way out of your way."

"This is new country to me. I got lost."

You don't know how lost. You don't know how alone.

"Come on," said Twist. "There's been too much yattering already."

He led the way back to the edge of the trees. Price and Burr followed him. The others were already working on the carcass. Presently they were hidden from sight. At the verge of the prairies the three men stopped and examined the visible world before they left cover. Price looked around and did not see anything and was ready to go on. Burr and Twist not only looked at earth and sky, they sniffed the wind and seemed to feel the quality of the air, like animals.

Twist gave a kind of shrug and said, "Well, we're in it now, whole hog." He began to run through the long grass toward the plane. Burr went fleetly after him. Price, oppressed with many things of which physical exhaustion was the least, ran heavily behind them.

When they were within perhaps fifteen feet of the plane a glittering thing came over the tops of the trees and hesitated, making a couple of short spirals in the air. Then it centered over the plane and hung there, high above. It was a disc-shaped object maybe three feet across, with a big lens on its underside.

Twist and Burr had stopped. Price came panting up to them. They were looking up at the disc, and Price saw in their faces a wild mingling of rage and hate and the despairing fear of men faced with an enemy that no amount of bravery or physical strength can prevail against.

"What is it?" he asked, and Twist said hoarsely.

"You must be from a long way west if you've never seen a flying-eye." His hands dropped to his sides. "Well. That's finished."

Burr began to curse at the thing. He looked as if he wanted to cry.

"What will it do?" asked Price.

"It'll hang there, right where it is, to guide the fliers from the Citadel. They can see us here where we stand, right now, in the Citadel." Burr's face was getting whiter by the second, like a man who has been stung by some venomous thing and realizes that in this present moment, between strides as it were, he must die. "They'll be starting. It's forbidden to come into the Belt. They'd kill us for that alone. But with the plane…God knows what they'll do."

"We can try and dodge them in the woods," said Twist, without hope. "Come on."

He started away, but Price said, "Can't we out fly it?"

"The flying-eye? It'll follow us like a hungry hound."

Some kind of television-scanner, Price thought, with a metal-detection unit and a signal relay to alert the main control in the Citadel. And what was the Citadel, and who or what within it was now watching him as he stood, and preparing for his death?

He said, catching the sudden terror from the others, "Shoot it down."

"Shoot it?"

"Smash the lens. Then it can't see us. Here, give me the rifle."

Burr said, "You crazy? No gun will carry that far."

"What kind of guns have you got?" said Price. "Damn it, give me the rifle."

Twist said, "Let him have it."

PRICE WAS a good shot. Not brilliant, just good. But today he was phenomenal. He blasted the lens and whatever insides there were behind it as fast as he could pump the cartridges into the chamber and fire them. He didn't miss once. And the disc flopped and slipped and crashed down sideways in the woods.

Price leaped for the plane. "Come on," he said.

The others were staring at him, with their jaws hanging open. "Did you see that? Did you see that gun?"

"Come on," Price yelled, "or I'm going without you!"

They tumbled in. Price started the motor, gunned it savagely, and took off as though the devil was on his tail. One of the men, he didn't know which, yelled out in sheer fright, once. Then they were clear of the treetops and climbing fast.

Price looked over his shoulder, and once again he thought he saw that dark metallic gleaming in the northeast.

"Which way?"

"Back across the river. And then," said Twist slowly, "I don't know. They've seen the plane. They'll come looking for it, and the first place they'll look is the Capitol, and after that the villages. They'll find it if it's anywhere near, and you can figure what they'll do to the people. They let us have our guns and our hunting knives, so we can kill game and even each other if we feel like it, but artillery, no. Explosives, no. And planes, no, no, no. Especially not planes. I don't suppose there's been one in the air for almost a century."

Twist shivered, his eyes shining, his hands gripping the seat.

"I'm glad I got to do this before I die. It's…" He fumbled for a word and gave up. "I can't say. But it makes you think what we were once, what we could have been today if it hadn't been for them." And he jerked his head back to indicate the direction of the Citadel. "The star-spawn. The damned Star Lords."

Burr looked out the cabin window. "It's an awful long way down." Then he asked Price, "Why'd you say you came to find the Chief?"

A suspicious man, Price thought, and so is Twist. Careful, careful. But how can you be careful when you don't know what's going on in the world, and you don't dare ask?

Price said, "I came to give him the plane. I'm the last of my family. I wanted to join up with somebody, and…there aren't many in the desert." This, he thought, was a safe assumption. "Life's too hard. I wanted to come where there are trees and water."

It was a good story. He didn't know whether they

believed it.

The Beechcraft left a fleeting shadow on the river and passed on. Twist peered anxiously into the sky behind.

"Can you go any faster?"

"I'm wide open now."

"Not fast enough. They come like lightning. *Whoom!*" Jets, thought Price, and began to look for a hole in the forest. Twist said, "And if they don't find us the first time, they'll send the flying-eyes."

"And they can smell metal," Price said. "So we've got to find a place away from any town and not only out of sight from above but also screened from a magnetic detector. Say in a cave, under a rock ledge, or close to some heavy concentration of metal they're already used to. Can you think of any place?"

There was a total silence, and he realized that they were looking at him with cold and bitter eyes.

"How do you know so much?" asked Burr.

"Isn't it obvious?" said Price impatiently.

"Not to us. What's all this about magnetic detectors and screens—and where did you learn it if you're not working for the Citadel?"

Twist laid the muzzle of the revolver casually against his neck.

"I wouldn't shoot me now," said Price, and explained why, very quickly. "Besides, that's a hell of a way to act. Just because I happen to know a little elementary science...how else do you suppose the flying-eyes find metal? By some supernatural method?"

"Hmmm," said Twist, and withdrew the revolver. "Maybe he's right, Burr. After all, we're hunters. We never studied much into those things." Burr grunted derisively, but he sat still, apparently convinced that there was nothing to be done about Price now. Twist thought hard for a minute. Then he said, "I know a place. There's a kind of a secret cave there, and room enough for you to land, I guess, figuring by what you took before."

He squinted out the window, confused by the differentness of how things looked from above. But finally he picked out a direction and told Price, "There."

After some low-level circling and searching Price found the place, a fairly flat stretch of bottomland in a little valley, beside an overhanging wall of granite. Twist's estimate of the room was hardly generous, but he made it, and taxied over bumpy sod as close as he could to the cave-mouth Twist pointed out. Then he sent the others to clear away some rocks and dangling creepers, and with a final heave and roar he managed to lurch into the cave itself. He cut the motor. He had about four hours flying time left in the tanks.

He got out of the Beechcraft and dragged stones under the wheels to chock it. Then he helped Burr and Twist rearrange the hanging vines over the entrance.

A high shrill screaming in the sky gave them less than ten seconds warning. They ducked back under the overhanging ledge and peered motionless from under it. And Price saw close above him, skimming the rolling land like an eager hawk, an ovoid craft that was not like any jet he had ever seen, wingless, leaving no trail, but tearing with a mighty shriek of power through the sky.

CHAPTER FOUR

TRAPPED in a strange dream, Price looked down from the forested ridge into a shallow green valley. Burr pointed and said,

"There it is. The Capitol of the Missouris."

He said it with pride. He and Twist had talked of this place, in the two days since they had hidden the plane and headed north. And they had talked of it proudly. Their home, the city of their people, the focus of a shadowy government that ruled the forest-lands which once had been two great states.

Price looked at it, and he felt pity. Pity, and a wrenching regret for what the world had once been, and what it had become during the lost years.

In the valley, straddling a clear little river, lay a half-dozen streets of wooden houses and workshops and smithies. The buildings were neat enough, of massive squared timbers. But the streets were un paved and dusty, and their only traffic was loaded wagons from the surrounding tilled lands, and pack-horse trains from the forest trails, and men, women, children in drab leather and wool. A faint sound of creaking axles drifted up through the drowsy afternoon air.

"The Capitol of the Missouris," Price thought. "And oh God, why did it have to happen to our world?"

He had listened, on the way here, to everything Burr and Twist said. Bit by bit, the jigsaw fragments of information had fallen into place, and a few casual questions had completed the apocalyptic picture.

It had happened long ago in the lost years, the years that Price had been hurled through. As near as he could make out the date had been 1979, sixty years ago.

That had been the year of doom. That had been the year when they had first come from outer space.

The Star Lords. The Vurna, as they called themselves. The accursed star-spawn, as men called them. Their tremendous cruisers had come out of the blue, had poised above the Earth, and then had struck.

Every city, every big town, every atomic power plant, every arsenal, every important bridge, viaduct, dam and factory. In one week of holocaust, they had been smashed by the remorseless cruisers that went round and round the planet. Millions died, that week. And the Star Lords' cruisers went away.

Quickly, they had returned. This time, not to destroy but to seize. What had been the fat, smiling lands of Illinois and Indiana, they had made their domain. In it, they built their Citadel.

The Citadel was a fortress, a city, above all, a base. The Star Lords contemptuously refrained from attacking the dazed Earth peoples who had been thrown back to near-primitive conditions. To the lords of the Citadel, Earth was only the site of an important base. Or so they said.

Was it any wonder, Price thought, that these men of the Missouris would kill anyone, anything, from the Citadel? Just hearing of it all had kindled his own rage. These mens' fathers had lived it, and they were still living it.

He looked down at the wooden town, as he and Burr and Twist went down a trail, and he thought, "Careful, though! They still think I may be from the Citadel—watch every word!"

Two hours later, Price sat in a wooden-walled room in the biggest of the houses, facing the Chief of the Missouris.

His name was Sawyer, and he was old. But he looked formidable as an old panther in his buckskins. His leathery face held deep pride, intelligence, and a brutal ruthlessness. Behind him stood the Chiefs of the Indianas and of the Illinois, those scattered peoples on whose lands the Citadel now stood.

SAWYER listened without a word to Price's story, and all the time Price told it he thought how thin and far-fetched it sounded. But, looking at these faces, he knew he could never convince them of the truth.

"Two days ago," said Sawyer finally, "the Vurna were here. They were almighty hot and bothered. They were looking for a plane. I never saw a plane in my life, and I said so."

He paused, his swarthy, wrinkled face brooding, and no one, least of all Price, dared speak.

He went on. "Since then, the sky's been lousy with their flying-eyes, hunting and hunting. You must have seen them."

Burr took that as an opening. "We did. We kept ducking them, all the way."

Sawyer looked out the doorway at the dusty, sunlit street and then back again to Price and he said with sudden blazing fierceness,

"You tell me you heard of us Missouris way out in your mountains, that you wanted to bring your plane to us...why?"

Price floundered. "Why, I wanted to help you..."

"To help us do what?" A garnet light was in the old man's eyes now. "What did you hear we were doing that you wanted to help on?"

Price sensed from the other's fierceness that he was in imminent danger, that something he had said had deepened suspicion.

He almost welcomed the interruption that saved him from answering now, though it was a sound that raised the short hairs on his neck.

The sound of shrieking power across the sky, the sound of

the sky-hunters from the Citadel...

"That's the damned star-spawn coming down here again!" said one of the men behind Sawyer.

The old man got to his feet with amazing alacrity. He rapped an order to Twist and Burr, pointing to Price.

"Take him upstairs. If he makes a peep, cut his throat...but do it quiet."

Little more than a minute later, Price was in a hot, dusty little room. It had gun-slots in its heavy wooden shutters, and they let level bars of golden light into the room.

He heard the whine of the flier, coming down fast. He went to the gun-slot.

"No," said Burr.

Price turned and looked at him. He kept his voice low. "The hell with you," he said. "You can stand behind me with your knife. I'm not going to yell. But I'm going to see."

He heard Burr and Twist come up close behind him, as he peered out the wide slot.

Out in the green square, a white craft marked with a curious insignia was making a vertical landing. He thought it was a type of aerodyne. He had never seen one in flight, back in that strangely far-off and quickly fading time from which he had come, but he had seen sketches and a working model. This seemed to be a refinement of the same principle, faster than a jet and maneuverable as a toy balloon. His hands itched to fly it.

He saw the insignia on its side—a golden sunburst with what looked like a many-colored, many faceted globe at its heart. He did not know what it signified but he knew what it was. The mark of the Star Lords, of the Vurna. And even as he looked, four of them came out of the craft.

They came along the street to where Sawyer and the other Chiefs and a little crowd of leather-clad men silently waited. No one had a gun; no one made a motion. Yet that dusty street was electric with a hatred so deep and strong and quivering that it made Price shiver.

Yet the four Vurna came straight on. The Star Lords, they from unguessable spaces who had smashed Earth like a child's toy, to make it their footstool. Price pressed closer to the gun-slot. He wanted to see them very clearly indeed.

Especially one of them.

THE STAR LORDS were tall and well formed, and they looked much like Earthmen except that they wore tight-fitting garments of various colors, but all cut to the same pattern. Price guessed that they were uniforms, with the colors indicating rank or branch. The other chief difference was the coloring of the Star Lords themselves. They were bronzed as though by radiations fiercer than any known on Earth, and their hair was silver. Not white, and not pallid, but a rich silver. The men—three of the four were men— wore their hair short.

The woman wore hers long, rippling onto her shoulders. It caught the sunset light and gleamed like hot metal. Her uniform was a deep crimson, duskier than flame, molding her long thighs and her high, just-full-enough breasts.

Sawyer was speaking to them now, his voice rolling out harshly in the silence. "If you're still hunting for that plane, my answer's the same. I've never seen one."

One of the Vurna men, who seemed to have the authority, stepped a pace in front of the other two men and the woman.

The woman had raised her head and was looking restlessly at the blank or shuttered windows of the timber houses. Price felt uneasily that she knew he was there and was looking at him through the gun-slot. But that, of course, was ridiculous.

"Sawyer, listen to me," said the man of the Vurna. He spoke clear but stilted English, with strong tones of some alien tongue in its unaccustomed rhythms. He wore a black uniform with a small gold sunburst at the collar. It was impossible to guess his age. And while he kept his voice quiet and his manner calm, there was anger in him.

There was anger in Price too, a deep rage growing in him as he looked at the men and the woman who stood here like conquerors on the planet they had ruined, indifferent to the hatred they faced.

"Here is no time and no place for stubborn obstructions," the Vurna man was saying. "Things move quickly now. We have an enemy before us so vast and powerful that we dare not have one also at our backs, no matter how weak. I ask you to believe that, Sawyer. I ask you to understand that if we Vurna fall, you perish—" he made a sudden chopping gesture of the hand "—utterly."

"I ask *you*," said Sawyer, "to look at my white hairs, and not insult them by talking to me like I was a child." His voice was strong, and anything but servile. "You can forget that old tale of the 'enemy.' I laughed at it when I was in my cradle. There's been only one enemy seen on this Earth, and that was you."

The crowd muttered, *Yes.*

"Your starships," Sawyer said, "smashed our cities and broke our nation and our world down to where it is. My own father saw it happen. One day a free world, the next— nothing. So fast there was hardly even a blow struck back. You did it."

The crowd muttered louder. Price felt Burr and Twist move beside him, breathing in the dark. Breathing hate.

"Don't come to me, an old man," Sawyer said, "and ask me to believe foolishness. As for the plane you say you saw, I tell you again I haven't got it. And if I did have I wouldn't give it up to you, nor the man either. And you know it, Arrin."

The woman spoke briefly in her own language to Arrin, her tone and gesture seeming to say that they were wasting their time. Her voice was low and clear, as beautiful as the rest of her, but there was an impatient contempt in it that made Price bristle. The same thing was in her eyes when she looked at the old Chief of the Missouris.

Arrin shook his head. "Sawyer, I tell you once more, as you have been told for two generations, it was not the Vurna who destroyed your world, but the Ei. And I tell you that the Ei may even attack the Citadel, and that the fate of Earth would be decided in that battle, just as much as ours."

HIS VOICE rose suddenly in very human anger. "There is a war, you stubborn old man! A war vast—huge—" His arm swung in a wide circle that seemed to include the whole sunset sky. "Beyond your comprehension. Earth is nothing in it. A forward base, an observation post, that is all. But if we lose it, the Ei will sweep this part of the galaxy and you will regret it more than we. We can withdraw. You cannot. You think you are cruelly treated now. You will weep to have us back!"

Sawyer remained unbending and unimpressed. Arrin sighed. His voice was quiet when he spoke again, but it had a ring of iron in it.

"I feel pity for your barbarism, until I remember that it continues because of your own proud stupidity. If ever you people of Earth had been willing to work with us...but let it be. And now I warn you, Sawyer."

He seemed to grow tall, grim, alien, the spokesman of inhuman forces. Price felt the skin grow cold along his back, and his belly knotted tight with the pricking of fear.

Arrin said, "If you are planning an attack upon the Citadel, forget it. We will slaughter you without mercy—not because we wish to, but because we must..."

Price caught the sharp intake of breath from the men beside him, and suddenly he understood many things he had not understood before.

Arrin was still speaking. "I will give you three days in which to deliver to me the plane and the man who flew it. If this is not done, we will be forced to use harsher measures. You understand?" Sawyer said, in a tone as cold as Arrin's, "Is that all?"

"One more thing. Keep your hunters out of the Belt. It is a military zone, not a game preserve. Any more incursions will be regarded as a possible invasion—"

Again Twist made a sharp, harsh sound in the darkness.

"—and we will make of it a blasted barren where not even a mouse or a beetle can survive. Consider that, Sawyer."

Arrin turned and walked away, the two men and the woman falling in behind him. Price watched the dark-crimson figure with the bright hair until he could see it no longer, and it dawned on him, as though the two things had a connection, that he was alive and living in this crazy world of Sawyers and Citadels and invaders from the stars, that these were his realities now and he had better wake up and grapple with them, or he would die—and the death would be for real, and not any portion of a dream.

The aerodyne took off with a scream and a whistle. The crowd in the square began to break up. Sawyer turned and came into the house, the chiefs and the sub-chiefs following him.

Burr opened the shutters and a welcome breath of air came into the stifling room, with a last gleam of dying sunlight. Price looked at his companions. They were watching him, their eyes sharp and hostile.

"So that's why you were so frantic for the plane," he said. "You're planning an attack."

Burr said fiercely, "You should've let me kill him when I

wanted to, Twist. And we should've left the plane where it was. Then they wouldn't have got suspicious."

"Maybe so," said Twist, and nodded. "Maybe so. On the other hand, if he *is* telling the truth, it might make all the difference."

There was a clattering on the loft stair, a man running up the steps. He came in and nodded to Burr and Twist.

"Sawyer says, bring the prisoner down—and hurry."

CHAPTER FIVE

SAWYER was standing in the middle of the room, talking rapidly to the chiefs of the Indianas and the Illinois. The Indiana chief was old and fat and lazy, but the Chief of the Illinois was young, heavy-jowled and hard-eyed, the type that is born suspicious and never gets over it.

Sawyer turned to look at Price. He was intent and wire-drawn, a man poised on the brink of great happenings, at that crucial point from which he may still choose whether to advance or retreat. Price bore his gaze steadily, and it was not easy to do, because the eyes of this tough old man seemed to be laying bare everything within him.

"But you can't take him *there*," said the Illinois Chief violently, looking also at Price. "The biggest secret on Earth, and if he's a spy…"

"If he's a spy," Sawyer interrupted harshly, "he'll never live to tell what he sees there."

He spoke to Price. "We're going on a journey. You're going too. And you two…" to Burr and Twist "… will guard him."

Burr and Twist nodded silently, and got their guns. The rifle and revolver had been handed over to Sawyer for safe hiding, and these guns were the clumsy, short range bolt-action rifles of their own handcrafting.

Price said, "This is a hell of a way to treat a man who comes to you as a friend. I hate the Vurna as much as you do, for what they've done to Earth, and"

Sawyer stopped him, saying ominously, "Save your words, you'll need them later. We've got a hard ride before morning. Let's go."

They all went out through a back door, except the old chief of the Indianas who was not going. In the twilight outside, there were horses ready.

Sawyer and Oakes of the Illinois led off, and Price followed with Burr ahead of him and Twist behind him. One man rode ahead of the whole party with a lantern made to shine down but not up. The flying-eyes watched of night, too.

The six horses went all night at a steady pace, single file along a narrow track that dipped and wound through the forest. Price felt sure, from what he had overheard, that they were riding toward some great secret council. He guessed that his fate would be decided there, and probably the fate of the rest of mankind too.

There was nothing he could do about it till he got there. Meanwhile he thought about a long-thighed girl in crimson, with her bright hair swinging on her shoulders as she walked. He wished he could have had a closer look at her face. It had seemed beautiful, a clear forehead and a fine chin, but it was the eyes that told you what a person was, and he had not been able to study them. Could she be as heartless as all the Vurna were supposed to be?

He thought she must be. His hate of the conquering Star Lords was rapidly growing. Before they had come, this dark, wild forest he was riding through had been rich farmland and pleasant towns. And when they had smashed all that, and built the Citadel to hold the ruined Earth, they had tried to make men willing captives by telling them that story of the Ei. It was the old Big Lie technique, but this lie had been too big for anyone to believe.

The woman might not be cruel. Arrin might be only a decent officer in a hard position. But all the same, they were aliens, despoilers of Earth, and he was an Earthman. These were his people—Sawyer, Burr, Twist, even the hateful and suspicious Oakes. These were the ones he would fight for, and with.

If they let him.

But they had to let him. He was the man with the plane. And as he rode wearily through the dark, he thought he knew the argument to use.

JUST BEFORE dawn, when the world was at its blackest and most silent, there was a challenge in the woods ahead, and the man with the lantern answered. Here and there among the trees other shielded lanterns flickered, widely scattered, and the woods were full of quiet sounds, the creak of leather and jingle of bridle chains, the soft thump of hoofs, the somnolent blowing of picketed horses. What men there were spoke in low voices.

Price's party dismounted and walked quietly among the picket lines. In a few minutes they reached the edge of the sheltering woods. The man with the lantern gave a low whistle, and another man materialized out of the blank dark ahead.

"This way," he said. "And watch your foot."

Now the man with the lantern followed him, the others coming after in Indian file. And Price began to see that the darkness was not as blank as he had thought. There were pale areas that gathered the faint starlight to themselves on flat, broken surfaces. He realized presently that these were walls, or had been once, and that he was walking on the shattered fragments of a city street. The feel of gritty concrete was unmistakable.

They went for quite a long way, apparently on some known path through the ruined city, and the sky began to pale before they reached their destination. Price could now make out the ghostly looming of building fronts on both sides, high fronts with nothing behind them, so that the window holes looked like a kind of elaborate pierced-work. It was deathly still, so still that their own breathing and the stealthy padding of their feet woke furtive echoes from the stone.

Their guide stopped beside a small black hole no different from all the other small black holes that lurked under fallen masonry and flattened girders. "Down there," he said, and left them.

They climbed down a wide steel stairway, bent and twisted, but mostly intact. A great wave of warmth from close-packed and steaming humanity rolled up the stair to meet them, mingled with the smells of candle-grease, smoke, leather, sweat and the lingering overtones of horse.

Beyond the bottom of the stair there was a comparative blaze of light. Price knew they were in the basement of what had been a public building or department store, a space foreshortened by a mass of rubble and hanging steel where part of it had caved in. It was crammed with men, and their voices growled in that low enclosed space like the growling of a great animal too long caged.

There was a small group of men sitting somewhat apart, and Sawyer joined them, with Oakes. Chiefs, thought Price, and realized that this was a very big council indeed, and planned for long ahead. Burr and Twist stood close on either side of him, but he forgot them for the moment, looking around in fascination at these, his countrymen.

Forest-runners and hunters, like Burr and Twist, in greasy buckskins. Men from the lower river, from the swamp and bayou country, soft spoken, hard-handed, dressed in coarse cotton dyed in bright Indian colors, yellow and red and green. Gaunt hill-farmers in hickory homespun, with their rifles between their hands. Boatmen down from the northern lakes, with a faint smell of fish about them, and long lean riders up from the southwest, leather-skinned and dangerous as rattlesnakes. Men from the black corn lands of Iowa, following their chief to talk of war. America, Price thought, basically unchanged, basically recognizable, but with all the fat sweated off it and all the luxuries stripped away, fined down to the ruggedness and strength of an earlier day, when men like this made a nation out of a wilderness.

He had a feeling they could do it again, in spite of the vast power of the Star Lords. And if they couldn't, they would go down fighting like wildcats to the last.

The Chiefs were talking among themselves. Twist knew some of them, leaders of the Iowas, the Michigans, the Arkansas, the Mississippis. Others they could guess at, Nebraska, Texas, Oklahoma, Louisiana. The two Missouri hunters were as excited as hounds before a hunt. Twist said there had never been a council this big in his memory. It would go on until the issue was decided, the men staying under cover in the ruins, the horses hidden in the surrounding woods.

PRICE REALIZED suddenly that the assembled chiefs were all looking at him with an intense and largely hostile interest. Sawyer's news seemed to have upset them badly. The Chief of the Michigans, a huge black-bearded man with an enormous voice, bellowed suddenly for silence. In seconds the place was absolutely quiet, except for the shuffle of men dosing in to see and hear a little better.

"Sawyer of the Missouris has something to tell you," shouted Michigan. "You listen hard. Because what he's got to say will make the difference whether we fight or hold our peace."

An astounded and angry roar broke out. Michigan jumped up on a makeshift stand and cursed them till they fell quiet.

"Do your howling afterward," he said. "This isn't just a whim on Sawyer's part. Something's happened. Shut up and listen."

Now they were alarmed and uneasy. They watched Sawyer climb the stand, their faces dark-bronze in the smoky light, their eyes glistening.

Sawyer said, "Twist...come up here."

Twist pushed his way to the stand and got on it. Burr moved closer to Price, his hand curled lightly around the haft of the knife in his belt.

Sawyer said, "Tell them." Perfectly at ease, aware of his importance but not impressed by it, Twist told the story of the landing of Price's plane in the Forbidden Belt, and what had been done with both of them afterward. He told only the simple facts, scrupulously avoiding any attempt to incite his listeners for or against Price.

The simple facts were enough. They heard them, the men of the Great Lakes and the southern bayous, the plains riders and the hill men and hunters and farmers, and their reactions were various and wonderful after the first shock of incredulous amazement. Twist had to stop to let the tumult die down, and when he could make himself heard again he said,

"Yes, it was just what I said, a plane, and I flew in it. Not one of those whistling fliers, but a plane...so." He made a graphic pantomime with his hands and a remarkably accurate motor sound. "Now I guess that's all," he said, and stepped back.

Sawyer said, his words carrying clearly to the farthest man, "The Vurna have turned our lands upside down to find the plane. They haven't found it. Last night Arrin—" A furious snarl greeted that name, so apparently it was well known, "— Arrin gave me three days to surrender the plane and the man who flew it. I've brought him here, instead."

He held up his hands, to quell the rising voices. "Listen— I'm not finished yet. Arrin had some other things to say. He said, '*If you are planning an attack on the Citadel, forget it.*' He said, '*We will slaughter you without mercy.*' "

"Now," said Sawyer, "here is what we have to decide. Two things. Is this man Price a friend offering us a weapon, or a spy of the Vurna offering us death? And shall we fight, or let it go until another year? They're big questions, the biggest you'll ever have to answer in your lives. Don't come at them like hasty boys, all feeling and no sense. Come at them man-like, slow and careful."

Michigan rumbled, "Those are good words. Heed them. And now let's have the man up here."

Burr gave Price a shove. "That's you."

Price shouldered forward through the pack and climbed the stand. As he did so Twist whispered in his ear, "Better make this good, boy. You won't get another chance."

His voice sounded friendly. Price was glad of it.

He stood on the platform and faced the chiefs and the representatives of the people.

Michigan said, "You tell your side of it. And speak up so everyone can hear."

Price spoke up, loud. But he said, "What's the good of that? I've told my side of it a dozen times already, and nobody believes me." He glared around the close-packed circle of men. "If I'd known you'd treat me like this, I'd have smashed the plane and left it for the coyotes."

"Just the same," said Michigan, "tell it again."

PRICE TOLD IT. "I didn't know you were up to anything in particular; it just seemed obvious that a plane might be useful to you sometime, now or later, and it wasn't doing any good where it was." He had coached himself so carefully in the story that it was beginning to seem like truth to him, gathering little embellishments and embroideries. "I brought guns, too, better than anything you have. And does anybody say, thank you? The hell they do. They accuse me of being a spy for the Vurna."

A low animal grunt from the listeners. Their faces were as hard as flint.

Price shouted, "Would the Vurna be so anxious to get me back if they'd just sent me out as a spy? You heard Sawyer."

The Chief of the Louisianas said, "It would be a very smart trick for them to say so, for just that reason."

"And how is it," cried the Chief of the Arkansas, "that right away the minute you turn up, Arrin says that about attacking the Citadel? Doesn't that show they know something, and want to know more?"

"I should think that was obvious," said Price. "There hasn't been a plane in the air for two generations. All of a sudden there is one. Wouldn't the Vurna want to know where you got it, and whether you're building more like it? And do you suppose they'd figure that with a weapon like that you wouldn't be planning an attack of some kind on them?"

That was good sense, and they thought it over, talking among themselves. Price felt he was getting somewhere, and marshaled his words for the final argument. Then the Chief of the Oklahomas spoke up and said,

"My word would be to kill this man and hand his body, and the plane, to Arrin. That way we comply, but not to his advantage. Arrin knows no more than when he started, but we look innocent. We look as though we have no use for a plane. And when their backs are turned, we go ahead as we planned all along."

And that sounded better yet, even to Price. Especially since he knew better than any of them the relative usefulness of one Beechcraft as a weapon against the kind of forces the Star Lords had.

But he knew if they began to think of that he was finished.

So he said, "Listen, you need that plane. It can reconnoiter, it can carry bombs—"

"Shut up," said someone fiercely. "Shut up, all of you. I hear something."

They quieted, and listened. Price couldn't hear anything but the tense mass breathing of the men. Then on the far side of the room first one man and then several began to dig like dogs after a rabbit into the heaped-up rubble.

"Here it is! Here it is...look!"

"What is it? Let's see."

"Ain't nothing but a little bitty box..."

"No! It's one of *their* contraptions. Let me through!"

A man in a linen shirt of green and yellow came bursting through the crowd, carrying something high over his head in one hand. He put it down on the stand, where it lay buzzing gently.

"Is that Vurna, or ain't it?"

Everyone drew back and away from it, as though fearing it might explode. It was a little metal box no bigger than a cigarette case, but Price knew what it was. He stepped forward and smashed it underfoot.

"You'd better clear out of here," he said. "Fast. That was a radio transmitter, broadcasting a steady guide signal to bring the Vurna right here."

There was one stunned moment of absolute silence, and then the place erupted into sound and movement. In the midst of it, in the heart of it, the Chief of the Michigans and the man in the linen shirt were possessed of the same idea. Crying "Spy!" they flung themselves at Price with their knives drawn.

REMEMBERING a trick or two the Army had taught him, Price stepped inside the chief's rush, caught his wrist, and flung him into the other, who had been slowed by the necessity of climbing onto the stand. And Price yelled at them furiously,

"Are you crazy? I wasn't near that side of the room. *I* didn't bring it and plant it here."

Twist stepped between him and the two men, drawing his own knife. "He wasn't, and that's a fact. Besides—"

"Get out of my way!" roared Michigan.

Unexpectedly, Burr leaped up and pulled him back. "I was close to him as his own skin, every minute," he said. "He didn't move, and he didn't have that thing on him to drop if he'd wanted to."

"We searched him," said Twist, "days ago. Personal."

"Then you're traitors too," said Michigan, clinging to his single idea. He started to charge again, and now there were others swarming up onto the stand after him, screaming for Price's blood.

Sawyer moved like a cat. Michigan halted in mid-stride, with the point of Sawyer's knife touching his heart-ribs.

"These are my men," said Sawyer. "I don't like having their loyalty called in question any more than they do."

Price leaned over and grabbed a rifle out of somebody's hands. He clubbed it and began to swing, scattering men like ten-pins off the edge of the stand.

"Get out of here, you fools!" he howled at them. "Can't you get it through your thick skulls? The Vurna are coming. Get out!"

Numbers of them were already streaming up the stairs. Now more and more took up the cry, seeming to understand suddenly that someone's treachery had made this place a trap. Sawyer said to the Chief of the Michigans,

"Go on, take that hot head back to the Lake and cool it. Hurry up, before they get you."

Michigan snorted like an angry bull, but he turned and jumped down into the crowd. The man with the linen shirt was gone. Price was about to follow when he saw the muzzle of a rifle, upflung, glinting darkly in the lamplight. He shouted to Burr and Twist to look out, "and then flung himself upon Sawyer. The shot was stunning in that closed space. He heard the slug go whistling overhead and then ricochet from the low concrete roof. Someone on the far side of the room cried out in rage and pain. "I thank you," said Sawyer, "and now let's get off this damned target."

They got off, the four of them sticking close together. Price did not see Oakes, nor the man who had carried their lantern. Most of the lights were going out, knocked over and trampled. The dark surge of running men carried them to the stair and up and out into full, blinding day.

Somebody pointed to the sky and yelled, "There they come—the Vurna!"

CHAPTER SIX

THEY WERE still a long way off but coming fast, whistling down the sky. Price could make out about a dozen bright dots flashing against the blue. Sawyer said,

"We'd better run for it!"

They fled, along the twisting path through the ruins. All around them, ahead and behind, other men were running, bolting away like wild creatures into the shadows of the broken walls.

And this was once their city, Price thought. A place of streets and homes and schools and churches, a good place, built with long hope and striving. What right did the Vurna have to break it?

He looked up at the fliers. They were larger now, moving swiftly above ragged crenellations that showed stark white in the hot summer sun. He looked down, and there was desolation. He ran in it, leaping and stumbling over the bones of a city, driven like the rest.

Sawyer swept a lean arm out in a commanding gesture. "Take cover!"

They dodged into the crevices of an unidentifiable mass half grown with creepers and rank grass. The old bricks tottered and threatened to fall as they pressed past them. They lay panting and listened to the Vurna fliers go over.

"They've broken formation," Price said. He had listened to hostile craft before. "Spread out. They'll sweep back and forth—"

A section of wall collapsed, close by them, with a rumble and a great puff of white dust. They leaped back, and Sawyer said, "That makes a beacon for them. Well, come on."

They ran out, crouching low, scurrying along the ravaged streets where their grandfathers had walked in peace. Price could see the green woods in the distance, but the air was full of the power-scream of the searching aerodynes, and he did not think that they would make it. He was right.

One of the ships shot down to hover three feet off the ground ahead of them, and another dropped behind. Sawyer turned to the right. A third ship came down. He turned to the left. A fourth one blocked him. He stopped where he was, too proud to look farther for escape where he knew there was none. Burr and Twist stood with him. All three lifted their rifles and prepared to die.

Price had nothing in his hands. The bright hovering ships mocked him, their noise deafened him, the wind of their air-blasts tore at him with vicious force. He hated them. He had never hated anything so much in his life, not even the enemy he had fought in Korea. He groped among the rubbish around his feet, half-blinded by dust and a red haze that was of his own making.

A loud metallic voice spoke to them from one of the ships. "Put down your weapons and stand together with hands high. You will not be harmed." Sawyer laughed. He hunched the rifle to his shoulder and fired. The slug went *splat!* on the skin of the aerodyne, and dropped.

"Put down your weapons and stand together. We will count six. At that time we will fire. Six. Five. Four."

Sawyer laid his rifle into the dust at his feet and straightened, folding his arms. Twist and Burr did the same. Tears stood in Burr's eyes, tears of outraged anger.

And this was their city, Price thought. My city. Ours.

Men began now to jump out of the hovering aerodynes, Vurna with cropped silvery hair. They wore uniforms of dark green. This was not their city; it was not their world. Price's fingers closed over an iron bar in the rubbish.

He sprang forward, holding the iron bar.

A BEAM of cold light, hardly visible in the sunshine, flashed out from the nearest ship. Price was running, and then he was not running, he was face down on the ground with the white dust in his hair. The bar spun out of his hand and fell with a faint clatter.

The Vurna closed in. They escorted Sawyer and Burr and Twist each into one of the ships. Two of the green-clad soldiers bent and picked up Price and carried him to the fourth. They clambered in, and the aerodynes rose whistling into the air.

Over the place from which the Earthmen had fled, roughly in the center of the city, several of the ships were gathered. They circled slowly, but nothing moved in the streets. At length all but one of them rose up, and that one made brief lightnings flicker from its underbelly. Down below a volcano erupted, thundered, burned, and died, sinking into ash and dust. That gathering place would not be used again, and any store of arms or powder concealed in it would not be used either.

The ships of the Vurna raced away toward the east. Behind them the forest was full of men and horses, moving out.

After a while a remote and disoriented consciousness returned to Price. He opened his eyes and saw a blur of red and silver and flesh tones. A little later he opened them again, and the blur had become a woman with silver hair and a uniform of dark crimson.

The woman.

She said, "You will be normal again in an hour or so. The shock ray does no permanent damage."

He looked at her, not caring very much about how he would feel an hour from now. He felt pleasantly languid, forgetful of his cares. Her eyes were a curious color, not like Earth eyes at all. They were like little bits of sky and moonglow and the far-off fires of stars, cool and strange and lovely. He said,

"They're not cruel, after all."

"What are you talking about?"

"Your eyes. They're beautiful. Like you."

A faint flush touched her cheeks. But she only said, "How are you called?"

He told her and she wrote it down. He saw she held a kind of clipboard on her knee. Just beyond her was a cabin window. Streamers of torn cloud whirled by it so fast that he was startled. Then other things began to impinge on his senses, air-scream, a smooth rush of speed. He sat up.

The man beside the pilot turned abruptly, his hand reaching for a weapon at his belt. The woman spoke to him in her own tongue, and then said to Price,

"We do not wish to stun you again. You will not make it necessary."

"No," said Price. He leaned forward, staring in fascination at the controls of the aerodyne, watching the pilot's movements.

"You are interested? As a pilot?"

"Yes." The controls seemed surprisingly simple. These controlled the force of the air flow, those the angle of the blast—"It's so much more maneuverable than a jet, and so much more powerful than any 'copter. I—"

He shut his mouth, abruptly conscious that he had made a bad slip. But the woman did not seem to have noticed it. He asked her hastily, changing the subject, "What's your name?"

"Linna," she said. "Of Vrain Four. That's the planet of a star in the Hercules Cluster. I have some other identifying words, a patronym much like yours and a set of code - numbers such as have been used on this world also."

"You seem to know a lot about us, for a girl from…uh…Vrain Four."

"That's my business. I'm a specialist in Earth cultures. Section 7-Y, Social Technics. Where is your home?"

She was friendly, almost too much so. Price was wary now, his mind shaking off the lethargy of the shock.

"Nevada."

She wrote on the clipboard, some kind of shorthand. "I have not been that far west. What is Nevada like?"

HE TOLD HER, leaving out any mention of cities. The aerodyne raced forward, and he watched the controls avidly. So simple. So beautifully, functionally simple. His fingers twitched with eagerness.

"You have flown a great deal?"

"My father taught me." Careful, Price thought. These people are probably no brighter or shrewder than my own, but they're better able to investigate and check on things. "Tell me, what's it like on Vrain Four?"

"We eat and sleep, make love and die," she said, "very much like you. The sky is very beautiful at night. The stars are close and burning, not cold and faraway like yours." She paused.

"Where did your father learn to fly?"

"From his father. It's a family tradition."

"And the plane had belonged to your family since the Ei destroyed the atomic cultures of your Earth year 1979?"

"Since the Vurna destroyed it…yes."

She did not argue the point. "How old was the plane then?"

Sneaky question, quietly asked. What was she driving at? Price began to feel that he was in a trap, but he could not quite see the shape of it. Then, before he was forced into an answer that might well be the wrong one, he saw something that gave him the perfect excuse to ignore it.

The thing he saw was a starship.

He had never seen a starship before in his life, but he knew this could not be anything else. He judged that they must be back across the river now and well within the Forbidden Belt. The ship stood like a tower of white metal, enormous, slim, delicate, a thing of slumbering power that caught the throat with awe and wonder. There were no trees anywhere near it, and the earth underneath was fused and hardened to a substance more durable than iron or concrete.

Linna said, "It's a reason we don't want men in the Belt. There's danger of being caught in a take-off or landing."

The aerodyne flashed past, and Price looked back as long as he could at the dwindling shape, splendid but curiously lonely in the middle of nowhere.

"I would have thought you'd have a port, close in. By the Citadel, I mean."

Linna shook her head. "Dispersal is much safer. That is why the Belt is so wide. We have a number of ships."

The man beside the pilot spoke, and Linna touched Price's shoulder, pointing ahead. "In a minute you will see the Citadel."

What he saw first was that iron blinking in the low air that he had seen from the plane. It grew with fantastic speed, taking shape, acquiring height and substance. Price had been prepared for something tremendous. In spite of that, he was wide-eyed and astonished as any tribesman.

The Citadel rose from a level barren, swept clear of every living thing. It was round, a vast flat-topped tower stunning in its stark hugeness. It did not fit on Earth at all. This monstrous, man-made metal mountain belonged to another world.

Around it as far as he could see were launching pads for a species of missile that looked more deadly than any of the

ICBM's they had been dreaming up in his own day. Atop the Citadel, on the vast plain of metal that was its roof, there were installations that looked like radar, and others he could only guess at—something in the radio-telescope line, perhaps, with elaborate grids. Set around the perimeter of the roof, and looking ominously out across the Belt, were hooded emplacements that made Price think of Arrin's warning: *We will make of the Belt a blasted barren, where not even a beetle can survive...*

"You see how helpless," Linna said, quietly echoing his own thoughts. "Men with knives and little guns—they would be throwing their lives away."

THE OLD ANGER came back to Price, and he said sullenly. "The Siegfried Line was supposed to be impregnable, too."

But he knew she was right, and he looked down with a sinking heart as the aerodyne swept in for a landing on the roof. How could Earthmen ever hope to throw this mighty power from their backs?

He stepped down to the iron deck, still a little slow and shaky when he moved. Other aerodynes were dropping down one by one. He looked around for Sawyer and Burr and Twist, but he did not see them. Vurna guards fell in on either side and Linna said,

"I think your friends have already landed, and are with Arrin below. Come on."

The invitation was pure rhetoric. He had no choice. The guard took him toward a circle painted bright red for the guidance of pilots, and about eight feet across. He asked, "Is Arrin the big boss?"

"The Supreme Commander of this base. You see how important you are to us...you and your plane?"

They stood on the red circle, and it dropped with them

smoothly down a gleaming metal shaft. It did not drop too far. They stepped from it into a corridor, brightly lighted by tubes sunk into the low ceiling. There were many doors on either side, and Vurna in uniforms of various colors passed back and forth.

The office of the Supreme Commander was as austere and functional as everything else Price had seen. Narrow windows with flush shutters of steel looked out across the sunlit Belt. One wall was a maze of screens and dials, communicator devices, and another had rows of tube-mouths with vari-colored tabs. Arrin stood facing Sawyer, with Burr and Twist behind their chief. There were several guards. As Price came in with Linna, Sawyer was saying,

"I told you I wouldn't give the man up, nor the plane. As for the meeting, your paid traitor can tell you all about it. And now you can go ahead and kill me."

Arrin said impatiently, "It isn't your life I want from you, but only a little cooperation." He looked up at Price, his eyes narrowing. "This is the man?"

Linna spoke to him in the Vurna tongue. A look of surprise showed for an instant on Arrin's face. He questioned Linna. Sawyer, meantime, said to Price,

"We thought they'd killed you."

Price shook his head. He was worried about what Linna was saying to the Commander. Once more he had the feeling of a trap he could not see.

Arrin nodded curtly, and gave some order to Price's guards. Linna said in English, "You are to come with me."

Price said, "I'd rather stay with my friends."

"Perhaps later."

There was no use arguing. Price went where he was told. On another and much lower level, which might have been underground for all he knew, he was ushered into a small, neat, impersonal cubicle with no window and with a lock on the outside of the door. Obviously, a cell.

Linna said, "I would like your shirt, please."

He stared at her. "What?"

"Give me your shirt."

Again there was no use arguing with her. He took it off and handed it to her.

"Food and drink will be provided," she said. "You will be quite comfortable."

She went away, with the guards. Securely locked in the cubicle, Price sat and brooded. Food and water came, packaged, through a slot device in the wall. He ate and drank, and brooded again.

Finally, Linna came back. She handed him his shirt and watched him soberly while he put it on. And then she dropped her bomb.

"You have been lying to me," she said quietly. "I know now where you came from."

CHAPTER SEVEN

PRICE STOOD stone still, meeting her gaze. But his thoughts were racing like startled deer. How could even the super-scientific Vurna have guessed his incredible origin? It was a freak, a fluke that wouldn't happen once in a million years...

Linna was saying, "Take your plane. Obsolete in model as it was, it would require extensive machine shops to fabricate it. And your clothing. Your shirt is of synthetic fabric, and so is the dye. It was woven on machines. And these are new—not relics preserved for a century."

Price managed to keep his voice level as he said, "So..."

. "So," Linna said, "there is somewhere a hidden community big enough to keep the old technologies of your people alive. A community we've known nothing about."

She regarded him in stern triumph, as though she had gained a victory.

Price sat down on the narrow bed. He had an hysterical desire to laugh, but he did not do that. Instead, he turned his head away from Linna as though to hide his dismay, but actually he was trembling with a sudden realization.

She had just given him his chance, if he kept his head and played it right. In her wholly mistaken, if quite natural, deduction of his origin, she had given him a chance for escape.

She misread his silence. "Further lies will not do you any good." Astonishingly, there was pity in her voice. "I see now what you intended. You wished to share your community's knowledge with other tribes, to give them new weapons in their fight against us. And now you hope still to keep your secret, so someone else may succeed where you failed. Believe me, Price, I understand—"

"Do you?" he said savagely.

"Yes," she said, her voice hardening. "And I understand better than you what would have happened to your army if they had attacked, armed with pitiful little planes like yours and only slightly more powerful rifles." She spoke swiftly to the guard outside, and then snapped at Price, "Come, I want to show you something."

She led Price out between the green-clad guards. They went down the echoing corridor of the cellblock, and into a lift that took them swooping up a long way, and then into another corridor and eventually into a medium sized room circular in shape, completely surrounded by a double row of screens. The lower screens gave a fixed view of the terrain within eyeshot of the Citadel itself. The upper screens reflected a roving, ever shifting view of the remoter Belt, the woods and prairies, herds of wild cattle grazing, deer bounding with their white flags up, the lonely starships waiting on their isolated fields. Four men in uniforms of dull gold watched the screens and checked a series of clicking recorders. Beneath each screen was a battery of studs.

"You see how much chance you would have of approaching unseen? And do you see what would happen to an army? One man here, touching those firing studs, and the whole Belt would become in seconds like the barren outside the walls. Nothing would be left. Nothing."

In Linna's eyes now there was the same impatient contempt for his stupidity that he had seen there before, when Arrin had talked to Sawyer in the square.

"And this is how you would help them…to their destruction."

If the situation had been what she imagined it to be, that would have been the truth. Price allowed a sullen doubtfulness to show in his face. But he said,

"What about your starships? You wouldn't destroy them."

"They can be flown on autopilot at a moment's notice, out of harm's way. Oh, for heaven's sake, Price, can't you see that I'm trying to help you? I don't want your people slaughtered. We, the Vurna, don't want them slaughtered. But if you persist in battering your stubborn heads—"

"All right, all right," he said crossly. "You've got the weight and weapons. Let's get out of here. It makes me sick to think how helpless we are."

THEY WENT outside into the corridor again. At its end there was a window, and Price stood by it, looking out. He pretended to be sunk in bitter reflection, but his brain was spinning furiously, trying to see all ways at once. He said,

"If I show you where our hidden colony is, you'll only smash it up. There's a lot there that isn't weapons, things that could help build up a civilization again. Why should I show you?"

"To keep some other idiot from trying to do what you have done. We won't destroy anything that's useful, only control it as to the production of weapons." She sighed, and added, "I hate to put it this way, Price, but if you don't show me willingly it will have to be another way, and I don't want that."

There was a real ring of sincerity in her voice. Price grumbled around a bit, permitting himself to be beaten.

"All right," he said at last. "I guess there's nothing for it. I'll show you."

"Good. I'll arrange for a flier—"

Her voice was drowned out by a sudden hooting of sirens all through the Citadel. For a moment no one moved. Linna's face became drained of all color. The guards stiffened, staring in a kind of wonder. The steel shutter of the window clanged to with a ringing snap, and Price could feel in that vast building a stirring and buzzing as of a menaced hive.

"What is it?" he asked, his feeling of triumph beginning to slip away almost before he had had time to enjoy it.

Linna's voice was quite steady when she answered. "Possibly nothing. You must return to your cell now. We'll discuss the trip later."

The sirens stopped.

The guards hustled Price along urgently now, as though they had more important things to attend to. The Vurna were shifting rapidly from places to other places, but all in good order. Only their faces were tense and they did not talk except to pass an order or ask for one. It was obvious that there was an alarm, that the Citadel was taking up battle stations, and that everyone was, if not afraid, at least severely uneasy. Price began to be uneasy too. Nevertheless, he noted the symbol that identified the floor, and studied the life controls as he was dropped down to the prison level again.

In perfect silence they stepped from the lift and started down the corridor toward Price's cell. Then the sirens screeched again, but on a different note. Linna gave a little sigh. Without thinking about it he put his arm around her.

"All clear?"

"Yes. What a relief. I'm technically a soldier, but I'm afraid a technicality is all it is. I...shh! Listen."

A clear metallic voice had begun to speak over some communicator system that apparently reached every corner of the Citadel. Linna drew away from him without seeming to notice his familiarity, listening intently. The guards listened too, and so did three or four other Vurna visible in the corridor. Price could understand nothing, except that the word "Ei" occurred several times. The Vurna's favorite bogeyman. He wondered if the Vurna powers-that-were used it to hoodwink their own people, too. It would explain Linna's sincerity, Arrin's honest annoyance, if they themselves believed in a menace called the Ei.

The window at the end of the corridor had reappeared as the safety shutter slid back. Through it, tantalizingly small and far away, Price watched the landing of a starship, and it was disappointingly remote and unreal as a scene done with models for an old film.

Until he felt the mighty fabric of the Citadel, man-made mountain of steel and iron, quiver underneath him with the shock wave of that landing. Then he knew.

The voice stopped speaking. There was a moment of dead quiet, as though what the voice had said was more momentous than the alarm. Linna's face was pale again, and the guards looked both excited and apprehensive. One of them spoke to Linna, and she shook her head, apparently giving him a reassuring answer.

Price said irritably, "Can you tell me what's going on?"

"There was a skirmish," she said, "out there. That's what the alarm was, to tell us there was fighting going on, but of course it was already over. There was only one Ei ship, a scout."

"Oh," said Price, and almost smiled. Scramble them once in a while, keep them on their toes. Remind them of the menace. It was a simple technique. Earthmen had evolved it quite early.

People were talking now. He could hear their voices echoing down the metal halls, excited, fearful. Several went to the window to crane their necks at the distant starship. And then the metallic voice began to speak again, very crisp and clipped.

"Maximum security," Linna said. "All corridors cleared, all doors and safety bulkheads locked. All off-duty personnel in quarters. Go in, Price." She pointed to his cell door. "I have to hurry."

The corridor was clearing like magic. Price hung obstinately in the doorway. "What now?"

"They captured the scout. They're bringing in two of the Ei—alive."

One of the guards shoved him in, and the door slammed shut on its magnetic lock.

Price lay down on the bunk. So they had captured a scout, and they were bringing in two Ei, alive. And everybody in the Citadel was ordered behind locked doors. Handy. Very. He was beginning to feel less hostility toward at least some of the Vurna. They were not so hardheaded and skeptical as the Earthmen. They believed, and the belief was keeping them here to man an outpost fort when they would doubtless much rather return home.

He found himself unaccountably pleased that he had an excuse to stop hating Linna.

He thought about the plan he had in mind until he went to sleep.

IT WAS difficult, in that windowless and practically soundproof place, to judge the passage of time. To Price it seemed like centuries. He slept, and woke, and ate, and paced around, and fretted between hope and a despairing certainty that Linna had forgotten all about him. He slept again, and was awakened from that sleep by the deep shuddering of the Citadel as a starship either landed or took off. He lay drowsily wondering what it was like to fly one of those mighty craft, traitorously wishing he was a Vurna so he might have a chance to find out, and dreaming of space and stars and foreign worlds.

The Citadel shook again, and yet again, and Price came wide-awake. He counted twenty-one, and there was no way of knowing how many landings or take-offs had occurred before he woke, or too far out in the Belt to be noticed here.

Certainly some large movement was underway. He took to pacing again, in a sweat of worry over what this meant, not to the Vurna, but to him.

After what seemed an eternity the door opened and Linna stood there, looking pale and grave. There were no guards with her. She was alone.

"The flier is waiting, Price," she said. "Let's go."

He joined her. And now he saw that the aspect of the corridor had changed. A sliding bulkhead had closed off part of it behind a wall of iron.

"What's that for?" he asked.

"Our—prisoners," said Linna, as though the word stuck to her tongue. "Come on."

She seemed in a great hurry to get away from that bulkhead. Price said, "What's the matter, aren't they human, or something?"

She gave him a look. "You still think it's all a great joke."

"I didn't say that."

"You mean it, though. You still believe the Ei are something we made up to shift the blame from ourselves. Probably you believe we are staging this whole matter to impress you and your chief, so that you will go back and assure your tribesmen it is all true."

This was so uncomfortably close to what Price was thinking that he said involuntarily, "You're entirely too smart for such a pretty girl."

"Sometimes I think," she said between her teeth, "that there is no hope for you people, no hope at all."

Price nodded toward the bulkhead. "The solution is simple enough, isn't it? Let me see them. Then I'll have to believe you."

"Simple enough," said Linna, echoing his words. "Do you think you could stand against them? We have fought them for generations, we have knowledge and experience, and even for us, with all our safeguards, it is difficult. Only a few, like Arrin, would attempt it, and I saw him this morning. He looks like a ghost."

"And that's why you've never let any Earthmen see an Ei—because they're too dangerous."

"No. It's more simple than that. We have had none to show. These are the first Ei we have captured for a century, at least in this sector of the galaxy. I have never seen one, either. And I don't want to."

She strode off, away from the iron wall across the corridor. Price shrugged and followed her.

"Where are my friends?"

"They're here," she said, indicating the row of doors they were passing. "Quite safe—or as safe as any of us. They'll remain here until…" She hesitated, and Price realized for the first time that she was deeply, genuinely afraid. "Until we see what happens," she finished.

"After that, what?"

"If they're still alive, and we're still alive, and there's still a world, they'll go free, and perhaps they'll be wiser men than they are now."

She would not say any more.

The lift swept them up to the roof. It was late afternoon, intensely hot, with storm clouds banking in the west. The roof area seemed almost deserted, and only one flier was visible. Linna motioned him into it and climbed in herself. She spoke to the pilot, and he took off immediately. There was no copilot. Only Price, and Linna, and one man. Price felt a secret surge of assurance, of power, like when you're riding a streak of luck and the dice can't fall any way but right. He sat quietly, looking out the cabin port.

He saw almost at once that the starships were gone. The whole Vurna fleet must have taken off, shaking the Citadel with their leaving. Probably most of the men had gone with it. The deserted appearance of the Citadel, the lack of guards, the lack of a co-pilot, all pointed to a skeleton force. *If we're still alive, and there's still a world*, Linna had said. Battle, somewhere out in the far reaches of space? Perhaps. Or maneuvers, or a show of force connected with some galactic game he would probably never know about. It was not really important. What was important was the fact that for the present the defenses of the Citadel were weaker, much weaker.

He sat looking out the port and covertly watching the pilot's hands on the controls. Linna had some kind of a side arm strapped around her slender waist. Probably a shocker. The pilot had one, too. He considered the problem, and the woods and prairies rolled back underneath.

Linna spoke suddenly, out of a long and somber silence.

"This mission is more important than ever now, Price, or I wouldn't have been allowed to divert even one man from our defenses. I beg you, for the sake of your own people, to play fair with me. If there's either help or hindrance in our rear, we must know it. The Ei—"

Now said something in Price's mind. He did not stop to question it. When you're riding a hot streak, let it ride. Never stop to question.

He rose and hit Linna on the point of her pretty chin.

CHAPTER EIGHT

SHE DROPPED in her seat without a sound. Price clawed for the weapon she had at her waist. But the abrupt cessation of her voice had alarmed the pilot. He turned around and then shouted something imperative in Vurna, his hand going swiftly to his own belt.

Price beat him by a fractional second. His hand pressed the trigger and the unfamiliar weapon crackled in his hand, and the pilot fell over, letting his own shocker go skittering to the deck. The aerodyne had not swerved from its steady westward flight. He had been sure, from what he'd seen of its automatic stability, that it wouldn't.

Price straightened up, breathing heavily with excitement. So far, so good.

He tied Linna's hands and feet securely with her own belt and his handkerchief, and then attended to the pilot. Linna was already beginning to stir, and he propped her up as comfortably as possible, smoothing her hair back from her forehead. He smiled suddenly and said, "I'm sorry. I really am. If there had been any other way, I wouldn't have done it."

He kissed her on the mouth, rather swiftly because he did not have much time, but with a full measure of feeling even so. She sighed, and he thought her lips answered his, but he doubted if that would be so when she came to.

He slipped into the pilot's chair and studied the controls, erasing every other thought from his mind as he remembered what he had learned from watching. The aerodyne was humming straight and steadily on. He had plenty of altitude.

He began to experiment, gingerly, and by the time he was

across the river he was satisfied that he could control the craft well enough to get by. It was considerably simpler than learning to drive a car in the old days, and he had a lifetime of flying behind him to give him air-sense. The craft itself was a thing of beauty, topping anything he had ever flown. He angled southward and westward, away from the river, traveling like a bullet.

Linna spoke from behind him. Her voice was very cold and very hard, the voice of a stranger.

"Arrin told me I should have you bound. I left you free on my own responsibility."

Price felt bad about that, and he said so. "Try to look at it from my side, Linna. I have to do what I can for my own people. If you were in my shoes…"

"Go ahead," said Linna. "Talk is obviously useless. I shan't waste any more of it, except to tell you—"

She told him, vividly, what kind of a fool he was, and what she hoped would happen to him before he led all of his fellow fools to destruction. Then she shut up and would not speak again, no matter how he tried to soften her rage.

The dark green forest, rough-textured like a wool rug, rolled back and away around him, and the sun was swallowed up in clouds. He strained his eyes for the clearing that would mark the Capitol of the Missouris. He was flying by dead reckoning. He had no compass bearing to begin with, and the Vurna instruments were useless to him. The pilot was beginning to come round, but Price knew better than to ask him for instructions.

It was a red light of fires burning on the edge of night that guided him down at last toward the timber-built Capitol. And now at last Linna spoke, because the pilot, looking out, began to yell frantically in Vurna. She translated.

"He says don't cut the downblast so sharply, or you'll crash. That lever…there, under your left hand…ease it back."

Price eased it. He settled down to a rough and ragged landing, just about where the Vurna craft had settled before, when he had been Sawyer's prisoner. Men came out of the houses and along the streets, to stand as they had stood then, to greet their hated overlords with silence and contempt.

Price jumped out of the craft and approached the fires.

THERE WAS a startled cry, and then his name echoed back and forth, and the men closed around him. They were inclined to be hostile, demanding to know where Sawyer was, and what had happened, and how he came to be piloting a Vurna flier. Price shouted for quiet.

"Sawyer's alive. He's a prisoner in the Citadel. So are Burr and Twist. You want to rescue them?"

That startled them. "Listen," Price started, and then he saw Oakes pushing toward him with a small determined-looking group of men.

"Stand back," Oakes demanded. "Stand back, there. This man is a traitor. He betrayed the council, he betrayed Sawyer. If you listen to him, he'll betray you." He turned to Price. "You get back to your Vurna masters. Tell them we're not going to—"

"Oh, shut up," said Price impatiently. "You're not chief here, and you never will be, no matter if you do leave Sawyer to rot in the Citadel." He took the shocker from his belt where he had thrust it. "I stole that flier from the Vurna, and I stole this, too. I'll use it on you if I have to."

Oakes looked ugly, but he hesitated, and Price said, "Some of you, if you want proof of what I say, go look in the flier. Go on."

Several men detached themselves from the crowd and went off at a trot toward the flier. Presently they began to whoop and halloo.' They came back carrying the pilot and Linna, who looked at Price with the utmost hatred.

"It looks like a trick to me," said Oakes. "They could have been bound on purpose."

Price said, "Does it look like a trick that every starship of the Citadel fleet took off last night? You must have heard or seen them, even at this distance."

"Yes," said a lean farmer, "streaks of fire in the sky before dawn. I was milking."

Others had seen them, too. And now a note of excitement crept into their voices.

"What's it mean? What's happened there? What are you after?"

"The Citadel is stripped," he said. "And I know where the fire control is that commands the Belt. With this flier I can land right on the Citadel without being challenged. I can take some of you with me, and we can knock out those weapons. You can walk right in, with no more opposition than brave men ought to be able to handle. You—"

"Price," said Linna, in a voice of absolute horror, "you don't know what you're doing. The fleet has gone out to fight the Ei. Arrin forced some information out of the captives—the Ei fleet is somewhere outside this solar system, and our fleet's out to intercept it."

The terror in her voice increased. "But if the Ei forces evade our fleet and strike directly at our base here—don't you see, only our great missile batteries around the Citadel can defend Earth! If you storm the Citadel, there'll be no defenses at all."

He said, "Linna, I know you believe in the Ei. Probably most of your people do. But you've never seen one, in a century no one on Earth has seen one. They're a myth, a political stratagem, that's all."

She shook her head, groping desperately for words. "Don't follow him!" she cried out to the men. "Don't listen to him. We're fighting for your lives and safety too. Don't be so mad as to stab us in the back now!"

They looked at her in the firelight, the flint-faced men who were weary of Star Lords. Then, without paying Oakes any attention at all, they looked at Price.

"He's right," drawled one of them. "The star-spawn have given us the lie about the Ei too long. Ain't a kid on Earth believes it."

Linna's head bent hopelessly forward, and she turned away. She still believes it, every word, thought Price. Poor Linna. He would have given anything to comfort her.

But there was no time for comfort, no time for anything but planning. He said,

"You've heard, you know this chance may never come again...are you with me?" And they answered *Yes!*

"All right," said Price. "All right, we've got to have a council, to make plans, and then we'll have to move fast to strike before the fleet comes back. Who are your leaders after Sawyer?"

Five or six men came forward, district sub-chiefs. One of them nodded his head toward the two Vurna.

"What'll we do with them?"

"Treat them well," said Price sternly. "They're your assurance of Sawyer's life." He didn't know whether they were or not, but he didn't want Linna to suffer even discomfort because of him. He added, "Make sure they don't talk to anyone, though. And remember, there was a traitor at the big council. You'd better all keep a lookout, for signals and communication devices. And now—let's talk."

THE COUNCIL lasted far into the night. Price's biggest problem was to persuade the tribesmen not to bring their guns.

"The metal-detector units on the flying eyes would spot you before you'd gone ten miles into the Belt, and I can't take the control room that far ahead. It couldn't possibly be held that long, and no matter how we might smash the weapon controls they'd have time to patch them up and use them on you. You'll have to infiltrate the Belt on all sides, keeping under cover, and get within striking distance before I land on the Citadel. Besides, against the Vurna shockers, your guns aren't much more use than your hunting bolos. We'll try and give you better weapons, once we're inside."

"Of course," said one leathery-faced sub-chief, "when you've got us and the Ohios and Kentucky's and the rest all in the Belt, it would be a mighty easy thing for you to give them word at the Citadel, and have us all wiped out at once, like that."

Price said harshly, "It's up to you, whether you want to take the gamble or not. If I'm on the level, you can take the Citadel and get the Star Lords off your back. If I'm not, you're dead, but you won't get a chance like this again. Make up your minds."

They made them up.

"How shall word be sent in time to the other tribes? It'd take days for a man on horseback to get around to the east and north."

"I'll take the word," said Price. "In the flier. By sundown tomorrow, there'll be men from every tribe ready to move into the Belt. And pick me half a dozen seasoned men to go along, under a sub-chief. Half a dozen men you can trust for the fate of the whole attack."

The leathery old chief, whose name was Sweetbriar, said quietly, "I'll pick you six, and I'll go along."

His gaze locked with Price's, and Price smiled.

"I'll give you the shocker," he said. "You can use it any time you see fit. And *that* should convince the other tribes they can count on me."

"Should," said Sweetbriar, nodding. "Now we'd better

reckon up our distance. As I see it, this'll work out something like a big beat, and if we don't all get there together, we might better have stayed home."

They settled all the details, the forced marches by night, the meager weight of food each man was to carry. Price managed to get an hour's sleep before he took off in the pre-dawn gloom to rouse the other tribes. When he slept he dreamed of an iron mountain, impregnable, crowned with destruction, watching incessantly with a thousand eyes. In the dream, he knew that no mere men could ever take it.

CHAPTER NINE

THE AERODYNE flew high in the black night, toward the Citadel. Above there were clear stars. Below there were heavy clouds laced with lightning, hiding the earth. Hiding the Belt, and the lines of men who moved in it, among the dark trees, in the wind and the rain.

One full night had passed, and another was drawing to its close. Before the sun went down again it would be all over, one way or the other.

Price was in that state of exaltation that comes at a certain point of prolonged tension without rest, where you move a little bit outside your body and above the ground, detached from every normal consideration, and everything seems to go with a clear headlong rush, as though a single initiating act has set an inevitable series of reactions going, and all you have to do is keep pace with them. He had not slept much, but he was not tired. The aspect of the Citadel roof, the round red circle of the lift and the controls thereof, the symbol marking the proper level, the shape and size and position of the fire control center, burned brightly in his mind. Their set and proper sequence did not permit of any obstacles.

Sweetbriar sat beside him in the co-pilot's place. He held the shocker in his gnarly hands, and from time to time he turned it over or stroked its smooth and unfamiliar shape. So far he had not had any occasion to use it. He had stood beside Price in a dozen wooden-built towns, helping him harangue a dozen doubtful chiefs, or sub-chiefs, around the perimeter of the Belt. He had not slept much, either, but his eye was brilliant and steely as a hawk's. If the sensation of flight frightened him, he had not shown it in any way.

The six men of his picking sat quietly in the cabin. They might have been the same six men Price had first met when he landed in the Belt, woods-rangers, hunters of deer and wild cattle, all speed and muscle, born fighters. They were as lax as idle hound dogs now, when there was nothing to be done. They, too, had mastered whatever fear they had had of flying.

The storm below was moving rapidly toward the east, over a broad front. Price could easily have outflown it, but he did not, only keeping high enough above it to get a sighting on the Citadel when it came into visual range. He was grateful for the storm. It seemed like an omen of good fortune. It would cover the advance of the tribesmen from the west, and it would cover his own landing, if he paced it properly. A thick night would make it easier to get his attacking party onto the lift, and perhaps even below, before it was realized that they were not Linna's party returning.

Poor Linna. He had seen her for just a minute before he left the Capitol of the Missouris. He had wanted to make sure she was safe and comfortable, and he had wanted to try once more to make her understand how he felt.

"I'm not your enemy, Linna," he had said. "Believe that. After this is all over—"

"If you take the Citadel," she had answered, "it won't matter who is anybody's enemy. You and I will both be victims of the Ei. If you don't take it...you'll be dead, and so will your crazy army, and how long will they let me live after that? Either way, both of us lose."

And she had sounded so quietly despairing that he had almost lost heart.

But not quite.

Starshine and the lower flarings of lightning showed him a gleam of dark metal far down in the night. He spoke to

Sweet briar and pointed. The old man peered, squinting, and the six hunters roused themselves and peered also.

"Don't look like much from here," one of them said.

Price did not dispute him. Perhaps it was just as well for his army of seven not to have too clear a look at the fortress they were planning to invade.

He hung for a little time in the high quiet air, watching the storm front roll like a wave. When it had almost reached the distant gleam of metal he said sharply,

"All right, *now!*"

And he dropped the aerodyne whistling down the sky.

THE WILD air currents caught him, boiling ahead of the storm and over it. For one horrible moment he thought he had lost control of the aerodyne. It pitched and skittered and tossed, throwing him against his seatbelt until his ribs cracked and his flesh felt as though it was cut through. The tribesmen were now frankly and vocally terrified. Then the built-in stabilizers and Price's own flier's brain took hold again, and the whirling-leaf motion steadied to a rough and racking but controlled descent.

He could not see anything now but the solid blackness of the storm clouds, until the lightning flared and lit the rain-swept barren below with a vivid light, brief but enough to guide him. He had judged carefully, and he let the main wind-drift carry him until the wall of the Citadel showed up huge and startling in the glare of a striking bolt. He hung rocking over the roof until another one showed him the painted circle of the lift. Then he set the aerodyne down hard right beside it.

There was no need for any talking. The instructions had all been thoroughly discussed before. Price and the seven tribesmen were out and across the intervening few feet of roof and onto the lift and going down before the next flare of lightning broke.

The men breathed heavily, their throwing ropes in one hand, their knives in the other. Sweetbriar glanced at the shocker. Then he gave it to Price and unhooked the weighted bolo from his own belt, swinging it gently.

There had been no alarm.

Price watched the symbols gliding past on the guide-strip. When the right one showed he pushed the proper stud and waited. The lift stopped. The automatic door slid back. They moved fast, out into the corridor.

Only one man was in sight, going somewhere with a sheaf of papers in his hand. He stopped, and his eyes widened, and his mouth opened. Price fired the shocker. The man fell down and the papers scattered all over the floor. Price began to run. His own shoes made a quick sharp patting on the plastic surface. The moccasins of the hunters made no sound at all. He counted the doors, and then turned for a last glance at Sweetbriar and the men. Their eyes were very bright and the edges of their teeth showed. Sweetbriar nodded.

Price flung open the door.

And it was easy, easier than he had dreamed. The four technicians in their uniforms of dull gold turned and stood startled and staring for as long as a man might catch his breath, and that was time enough. Bolos wrapped around three of them like flying snakes and brought them down, and the fourth fell under the shock-beam.

"Shut the door," said Price, and one of the hunters shut it.

Price knocked out the other three with the shocker, and the hunters bound them. There was a rack of sidearms in one wall, with several shockers in it. Price handed them out and then turned his attention to the batteries of firing-studs. The hunters stood staring at the moving pictures of the stormy Belt reflected in the scanner screens, until Sweetbriar sent them to guard the door.

There were service hatches below the waist-high control panels. Price got one open and studied the wiring, panting more with excitement than exertion. It was only a few minutes until the prearranged time of attack. But he must not trip the firing relays accidentally in trying to deactivate them. He was afraid to start pulling wires indiscriminately.

But where the individual leads ran back to join the primary cable they passed through a series of switches. It seemed logical to Price that these were safety cutoffs to be used during maintenance, and that they would cut off the nameless destructive engines on the roof.

He had nothing better to go on, and time had almost run out. He opened one of the switches, and glanced swiftly at the screens. Nothing happened. He flipped open the others fast, and ripped the wires loose from the board. Then with a metal chair he smashed the studs.

As he finished, Sweet briar shouted suddenly. "There they come—and right on time!"

Price, sweating, looked up. Sweetbriar and the hunters were eagerly gazing at the screens.

They showed the storm-swept Belt and they showed small dark figures in it—hundreds of them—thousands—tribesmen running toward the Citadel.

An alarm bell rang somewhere in the Citadel. Instantly other bells echoed it, a distant confusion of alarms.

"Out of here fast," Price cried. "This is the first place the Vurna will be coming. If we can get down through, we can help the others."

They ran back out of the room, back down the corridor past the unconscious man who still lay on the floor. Whatever happened now, the tribesmen pouring across the Belt were safe from the weapons on the roof.

Without warning the lift-door opened right in front of them and five green-clad Vurna came spilling out of it.

There was no chance to use shockers or bolos either—they were so close to each other that it was hands and fists. They struggled, gripping and striking at each other, their feet slipping on the smooth floor, with the clamor of bells in the background.

A new note was added to that clamor. A dim sound of yelling voices, many of them surging up from the lower part of the Citadel.

"The tribes are in!" shouted Sweetbriar. "By God, I—"

HE WAS KNOCKED back by a flailing green arm. His Vurna antagonist scrabbled to get his shocker out of his belt. Price desperately kicked out at his own personal foe and banged him back against the metal wall. He saw the silver head bang the wall, and the man sagged at the knees.

Price rushed and knocked up the shocker now leveled at Sweetbriar. The hunters yelped, their eyes blazing. It was their kind of a fight. They liked it. After a sullen lifetime, they were using their fists on the Star Lords and they liked that.

The surge of sound from levels underneath told of a far bigger melee down there, spreading through the Citadel. And then that sound, and the small, personal noises of their own staggering fight, were cut across by a brutal authoritative new sound.

A hooting, loud and commanding, getting louder by the second, braying like the voice of doom through the vast iron pile.

The two Vurna still left on their feet tried to turn and run down the corridor. The hunter's bolos brought them down quickly.

Sweetbriar's leathery old face was wild and startled as he got to his feet. "What the hell—"

"That's the Vurna's big battle stations siren." Price said.

"They're a bit late with it. Come on!"

He and the hunters began to look for stairs, racing swiftly along the deserted corridors. They found some at last, and sped downward, level after level.

Bellowing, deafening in volume now, the siren kept hooting.

It could not drown out the tumultuous uproar that filled the lower levels. Price and the hunters were met suddenly by a mass of tribesmen boiling up from the ground level. They were screaming, laughing, capering in the halls, dragging with them one or two captured Vurna—triumphant victors, dancing down a hated power under their moccasined feet. Their hair and beards and their clothing were still dripping wet with rain.

They swept up Price and Sweetbriar and the six others in their advancing front, pounding their shoulders, hugging them.

"We did it! We got 'em!" they cried. "We took the Citadel!"

"Is it all over?" asked Price incredulously. "So soon?"

"That mighty caterwauling did it," said a red-bearded man. "All of a sudden they quit fighting and began to run, like it was a signal, but they couldn't get away from us. I heard they got old Arrin himself down there, in a big room, cussing and crying fit to bust."

"Where's Sawyer?" somebody shouted, and Sweetbriar took up the cry. Price said,

"Somewhere on this level, I think. Get a Vurna that speaks English and make him show you. It'll save time."

He pushed on through them to the stairs, and fought his way down. He wanted to see Arrin. He wanted to see the pride of the Citadel humbled, broken.

Tribesmen rioted through the corridors, smashing things like happy children. They directed him to a vast sunken room that Price knew must be the very heart and soul of the Citadel, its reason for being. It was an overpowering place of screens and towering panels and complex equipment. But these screens looked far beyond Earth, showing starry spaces, burning suns and unimaginable dark abysses. From here the Vurna had watched the whole sector of outer space, and these complex controls must be the triggers of the mighty missile batteries outside the Citadel, the weapons that could strike fast and far into the void.

Here there was a guard to keep out the roisterers. The soberer of the tribesmen had a sensible concern for the possible results of tampering with these incomprehensible but obviously mighty powers. They were afraid the whole Citadel might blow up with them in it. A few technicians were still being hustled out as Price entered.

A number of the chiefs were in here, and Arrin was with them, but he was neither cursing nor crying. He was standing between two muscular tribesmen, facing the chiefs, and his face held such an agony of despair and terror that Price was shaken by it.

"What must I do," he was saying, *"to make you understand?* That warning came from our fleet. The Ei have evaded it in the Centaurus Gulf, and are sweeping in toward Earth. If we don't defend the Citadel..."

He broke off as he saw Price come up. Then he said bitterly, "I congratulate you. Few men can say that practically single-handed they destroyed a world."

One of the chiefs asked Price, "Is Sawyer with you?"

Price shook his head. "They've gone to free him now. He'll be here in a few minutes."

"Oh my God," said Arrin softly. "Don't let them free the Ei. Even two of them at large here—we'd have no hope at all, with their fleet coming." He looked at Price and Price's confident scorn drained slowly out of him leaving a nasty void. Nobody, Vurna or not, could counterfeit what he saw in Arrin's eyes.

"Do you wish me to go on my knees and beg?" whispered Arrin. "I'll do it. Only go up and stop them from opening that bulkhead."

And Price knew suddenly that he must do that.

HE TURNED and ran back along the hall and up the stairs, pushing and kicking his way past the knots of tribesmen who wanted to congratulate him for what he had done, and all the way there was a chill unpleasant thing riding his back, and its first name was Doubt, and its second, Fear.

Was it possible, just barely possible, that the Vurna had been telling the truth all the time?

Uproar on the prison level guided him through a maze of corridors, to an obligato of breaking doors. He turned a corner. Burr and Twist and Sawyer were free. They formed part of the forefront of a group that was swarming down the hall systematically breaking down the cell doors. Two Vurna guards lay prone, and a third man, probably the English-speaking guide, was trying to crawl away unnoticed, his face ashen with fear.

The bulkhead was open.

A man's voice neighed suddenly in terror. Then another, and another, and the tribesmen were rolled back upon themselves as by the blow of a great hand, as the fore edge of the group turned and burst its way to the rear. There was a moment of wild panic. Price stood flat against the wall and watched brave men run by him sobbing. And then a wave of force, so cold and alien that it revolted the last small atom of his human self, hit his mind like the back-blast of a bomb.

Two dark forms stood in the corridor.

They were taller than men. At first Price thought they were shrouded in black like old monks, with cowls over their heads. But as they moved he saw that the cowls and the floating draperies edged with a thin translucent gray were their own substance, quivering, shifting, gliding around some unguessable central core of being. He could not see whether they had faces under the black folds, and eyes in the faces, but he could feel them watching him. He could feel their minds stripping him and tearing away his feeble defenses, leaving his own mind naked and helpless before them.

And these were the Ei. These were the Big Lie of the Vurna.

Only they were real!

He could not stand them any longer. He ran.

They all ran. It was a compulsion. Run. Cry panic. Clear the Citadel and get away!

He looked back and the Ei were behind them, gliding soundlessly along the hall.

Run. Get away...

And then Price and the others, fleeing in the next corridor collided with the chiefs who were hurrying to find out what had happened. They still had Arrin with them, a prisoner.

"Out," said Sawyer thickly, his voice a hoarse croak. "Get out, fast—"

Arrin's voice cracked like a silver whiplash. "Yes, run. Because they're making you, because their minds are too much for you! Run, and let them have the Citadel, and when their fleet comes, let them have the Earth!"

That stopped them. The horror they felt at that thought surged up so strong that the frantic compulsion to flee lessened a little. But behind them, somewhere back in the corridors, they would be following...

Arrin raged and mocked them. *"We* saved you from the Ei two generations ago, when Ei ships had smashed your defenses and they were ready to move in. We moved in first, we've held them back, but now you've let them in! So run!"

"Good God!" said Sawyer, his face stricken. "Then it was all true, what you told us about the Ei. It was true all the time!"

PRICE DID NOT, like the other Earthmen, have a lifetime's thinking to revise. He grabbed Arrin's shoulders.

"Can we face them?" he cried. "Can we kill them?"

"They can be killed," Arrin said. "Their minds can hold many, but not an unlimited number. If we all rush them, many of us, there is a chance…"

Price yelled down the corridors, "What are you running from? There's only two of them. We're going back! We're going to pull them down!"

The tribesmen, their first horror a little abated, by sheer reaction from shame of their own terror, exploded into sudden rage.

"There's only two of them—come on!"

And then of a sudden they were all of them running back down the corridors, jostling, crowding, screaming, Price with Arrin beside him, with old Sweetbriar ahead, with Sawyer shouting in hoarse anger. A mob, not an army, a mob urged forward by its own horror.

Around the corner, and into the corridor where the two black shapes came gliding fast. And it was like walking into night and death, into bitter black winds and the stabbing of cruel swords, as the might of alien minds blasted at them.

Tribesmen screamed and fell, clawing at their own heads. The mass behind forced over them, forced the reeling first wave right into the unimaginable shapes.

"Pull them down!"

Price was in the screeching forefront now and he closed his eyes and struck with his knife at the cloudy darkness of a cowl.

A cold like that of outer space struck through him and he

staggered, fainting and falling, and his mind closed on the awful sight of packed men swaying and pulling and striking at the two tall cowled shapes, mobbing them, beating them down.

When Price opened his eyes he was in another corridor and old Sawyer was slapping his face with rough hands.

"Yes," said Sawyer thickly. "They're dead. And a good many men dead with them, and some others that act like their brains are dead."

He shook his head, a little wildly. "To think it was true all the time—"

Whoom! came a deep sound from outside the Citadel. And then more of them, in quick succession. *Whoom! Whoom! Whoom!*

"Arrin…" said Price, getting weakly to his feet.

"He's down in that room, with his men," said Sawyer. "And they're turning loose on that Ei fleet out in space."

And now the great missiles from the launchers outside the Citadel were going out so fast that the sounds of them could not be counted.

Price said, "Then you let him…"

"Let him?" repeated Sawyer. "We *asked* him! Do you think we want a whole fleet of—of them—reaching Earth?"

By the time Price and Sawyer got down to the missile control room, the deadly messengers were all on their way.

Arrin and his men watched the screens, and would not turn from them. Price, and the tribesmen, saw only burning stars and dark space in those screens—and then, finally, a little crackling of pin-prick flares running like a swarm of fireflies in the dark void. Then nothing.

Arrin turned.

Sawyer said, painfully, "Did they…?"

"Yes," said Arrin. "We caught them—but none too soon. Our fleet out there will mop up any Ei ships that survived."

He added, with slow weariness, "We've won a battle—not a war. The Ei are many. But this outpost world is safe. And we'll press them back and back…"

Sawyer looked at Price. Price said, "Don't be so damned proud. Go ahead and say it."

Sawyer said to Arrin, "Seems like we were wrong about some things. About you Vurna. We're hoping things'll be different between us, now."

"They can be," Arrin said.

"They will be, if you want it." The old Chief of the Missouris asked, "Now it's all cleared up, just who was the traitor among us? Was it Oakes?"

For the first time, a little smile touched Arrin's face. "Do you really want to know, now it's over?"

Sawyer grunted. "Guess not." He looked around the other chiefs, and then stuck his gnarled hand out in the oldest gesture of Earth, and Arrin took it.

PRICE AND LINNA stood next day on the roof of the Citadel and watched the tribesmen going home.

There was, there had always been, a stiff-necked pride in the men of Earth. They went away with their heads up, not looking back. But, at the edge of the distant forest, there was a face turned and the flash of a hand wave before they went into the trees.

"They'll come back," Price said. "A few of them at first—then more and more, to learn. A few years will make all the difference."

He thought that the sons of Earth and the sons of the stars would together stand upon many far worlds. The long war against the Ei would end some day, that dark and alien tide would be rolled back, and Earthmen would do their share. But that was all to come.

Linna was saying earnestly, "And the people of your own

hidden colony in the west—they will join us too?"

Price looked at her. "There is no colony, Linna. I came alone from the west."

"But your clothes…your plane…where did you come from?" She was startled, her eyes wide and wondering.

"I'll explain all that later. You won't believe it, at first. I hardly do myself."

And, thinking of the strange freak of force and chance that had snatched him from the older Earth, Price felt a last pang of nostalgia for that lost world of long ago. That time when, safe on their cozy little planet, men had dreamed of space and stars—it seemed now like a long-dead idyll of youth.

The Earth of those days could never come again. The wider galaxy had crashed in upon it, and terrible and magnificent realities had shattered the youthful dreams, and it was a different and sterner planet that was joining the community of star worlds. Who knew what awaited it on that wider, cosmic stage? His hand tightened on Linna's. Of their own tiny part in that vast future, he felt suddenly very sure.

THE END

FIRST STOP MARS, THEN ON TO THE END OF THE GALAXY...

Temple was faced with an unpleasant, yet exciting proposition. He would be leaving the Earth—and the girl he had long been in love with—for a long voyage into the vast darkness of outer space. He knew it was a voyage from which there would be almost no chance of ever returning. However, little did he know that the future of the Earth itself rested completely on his shoulders. It started out with a trip to Mars and from there went straight on to the very ends of the known Galaxy.

Here is a wildly entertaining, intrigue-filled space adventure from one of the best known—and certainly most highly underrated—authors of science fiction's golden age, Milton Lesser.

CAST OF CHARACTERS

CHRISTOPHER "KIT" TEMPLE
His life—as he had known it—was over when he was selected for the government's Nowhere Journey. His destination was unknown even to his superiors.

STEPHANIE ANDREWS
She had the misfortune of loving a man who was leaving on a long, long space voyage—and never coming back!

ALARIC ARKALION, III
This son of a billionaire was a young man in his early twenties, yet there was something strange about his middle-aged eyes and his elderly wisdom.

SOPHIA PETROVITCH
She was the first Soviet woman to volunteer for a flight into endless space. Little did she know that mother Russia planned to transform her into a superwoman.

JASON TEMPLE
He was Kit Temple's brother and the town coordinator for Earth City. His only problem was that Earth City was located on the other side of the galaxy!

MRS. DRAPER
A political activist back home on Earth, she helped make it possible for a woman to finally make it to the stars.

ALARIC ARKALION, III
Now just wait a minute…this person was already listed above—or was he?

VOYAGE TO ETERNITY

By
MILTON LESSER

ARMCHAIR FICTION
PO Box 4369, Medford, Oregon 97504

CHAPTER ONE

WHEN the first strong sunlight of May covered the tree-arched avenues of Center City with green, the riots started.

The people gathered in angry knots outside the city hall, met in the park and littered its walks with newspapers and magazines as they gobbled up editorial comment at a furious rate, slipped with dark of night through back alleys and planned things with furious futility. Center City's finest knew when to make themselves scarce: their uniforms stood for everything objectionable at this time and they might be subjected to clubs, stones, taunts, threats, leers—and knives.

But Center City, like most communities in United North America, had survived the Riots before and would survive them again. On past performances, the damage could be estimated, too. Two hundred fifty-seven plate glass windows would be broken, three hundred twelve limbs fractured. Several thousand people would be treated for minor bruises and abrasions, Center City would receive half that many damage suits. The list had been drawn clearly and accurately; it hardly ever deviated.

And Center City would meet its quota. With a demonstration of reluctance, of course. The healthy approved way to get over social trauma once every seven hundred eighty days.

*　　*　　*

"Shut it off, Kit. Kit, please."

The telio blared in a cheaply feminine voice, "Oh, it's a long

VOYAGE TO ETERNITY

By

Milton Lesser

Temple faced leaving Earth — and the girl he loved — if his country drafted him. But the hard part was in knowing he'd never return! . . .

way to nowhere, forever. And your honey's not coming back, never, never, never..." A wailing trumpet represented flight.

"They'll exploit anything, Kit."

"It's just a song."

"Turn it off, please."

Christopher Temple turned off the telio, smiling: "They'll announce the names in ten minutes," he said, and felt the corners of his mouth draw taut.

"Tell me again, Kit," Stephanie pleaded. "How old are you?"

"You know I'm twenty-six."

"Twenty-six. Yes, twenty-six, so if they don't call you this

time, you'll be safe. Safe, I can hardly believe it."

"Nine minutes," said Temple in the darkness. Stephanie had drawn the blinds earlier, had dialed for soundproofing. The screaming in the streets came to them as not the faintest whisper. But the song that became briefly, masochistically popular every two years and two months had spoiled their feeling of seclusion.

"Tell me again, Kit."

"What."

"You know what."

He let her come to him, let her hug him fiercely and whimper against his chest. He remained passive although it hurt, occasionally stroking her hair. He could not assert himself for another—he looked at his strap chrono—for another eight minutes. He might regret it, if he did, for a lifetime.

"Tell me, Kit."

"I'll marry you, Steffy…in eight minutes, less than eight minutes, I'll go down and get the license. We'll marry as soon as it's legal."

"This is the last time they have a chance for you. I mean, they won't change the law?"

Temple shook his head. "They don't have to. They meet their quota this way."

"I'm scared."

"You and everyone else in North America, Steffy."

She was trembling against him. "It's cold for June."

"It's warm in here." he kissed her moist eyes, her nose, her lips.

"Oh God, Kit. Five minutes."

"Five minutes to freedom," he said jauntily. He did not feel that way at all. Apprehension clutched at his chest with tight, painful fingers, almost making it difficult for him to breathe.

"Turn it on, Kit."

HE dialed the telio in time to see the announcer's insincere smile. Smile seventeen, Kit thought wryly. Patriotic sacrifice.

"Every seven-hundred eighty days," said the announcer, "two hundred of Center City's young men are selected to e serve their country for an indeterminate period regulated rigidly by a rotation system."

"Liar!" Stephanie cried. "No one ever comes back. It's been thirty years since the first group and not one of them…"

"Shhh," Temple raised a finger to his lips.

"This is the thirteenth call since the inception of what is popularly referred to as the Nowhere Journey," said the announcer. "Obviously, the two hundred young men from Center City and the thousands from all over this hemisphere do not in reality embark on a Journey to Nowhere. That is quite meaningless."

"Hooray for him," Temple laughed.

"I wish he'd get on with it."

"No, ladies and gentlemen, we use the word Nowhere merely because we are not aware of the ultimate destination. Security reasons make it impossible to…"

"Yes, yes," said Stephanie impatiently. "Go on."

"…therefore, the Nowhere Journey. With a maximum-security lid on the whole project, we don't even know why our men are sent, or by what means. We know only that they go somewhere and not nowhere, bravely and not fearfully, for a purpose vital to the security of this nation and not to slake the thirst of a chessman of regiments and divisions.

"If Center City's contribution helps keep our country strong, Center City is naturally obligated…"

"No one ever said it isn't our duty," Stephanie argued, as if the announcer could indeed hear her. "We only wish we knew something about it—and we wish it weren't forever."

"It isn't forever," Temple reminded her. "Not officially."

"Officially, my foot. If they never return, they never return. If there's a rotation system on paper, but it's never used, that's not a rotation system at all. Kit, it's forever."

"...to thank the following sponsors for relinquishing their time..."

"No one would want to sponsor *that,*" Temple whispered cheerfully.

"Kit," said Stephanie, "I—I suddenly have a hunch we have nothing to worry about. They missed you all along and they'll miss you this time, too. The last time, and then you'll be too old. That's funny, too old at twenty-six. But we'll be free, Kit. Free."

"He's starting," Temple told her.

A large drum filled the entire telio screen. It rotated slowly, from bottom to top. In twenty seconds, the letter A appeared, followed by about a dozen names. Abercrombie, Harold. Abner, Eugene. Adams, Gerald. Sorrow in the Abercrombie household. Despair for the Abners. Black horror for Adams.

The drum rotated.

"They're up to F, Kit."

Fabian, Gregory G...

Names circled the drum slowly, like viscous alphabet soup. Meaningless, unless you happened to know them.

"Kit, I knew Thomas Mulvany."

N, O, P...

"It's hot in here."

"I thought you were cold."

"I'm suffocating now."

R, S...

"T!" Stephanie shrieked as the names began to float slowly

up from the bottom of the drum.

Tabor, Tebbets, Teddley...

Temple's mouth felt dry as a ball of cotton. Stephanie laughed nervously. Now—or never. Never?

Now.

Stephanie whimpered despairingly.

TEMPLE, CHRISTOPHER.

"SORRY I'm late, Mr. Jones."

"Hardly, Mr. Smith. Hardly. Three minutes late."

"I've come in response to your ad."

"I know. You look old."

"I am over twenty-six. Do you mind?"

"Not if you don't, Mr. Smith. Let me look at you. Umm, you seem the right height, the right build."

"I meet the specifications exactly."

"Good, Mr. Smith. And your price."

"No haggling," said Smith. "I have a price that must be met."

"Your price, Mr. Smith?"

"Ten million dollars."

The man called Jones coughed nervously. "That's high."

"Very. Take it or leave it."

"In cash?"

"Definitely. Small unmarked bills."

"You'd need a moving van!"

"Then I'll get one."

"Ten million dollars," said Jones, "is quite a price. Admittedly, I haven't dealt in this sort of traffic before, but—"

"But nothing. Were your name Jones, really and truly Jones, I might ask less."

"Sir?"

"You are Jones exactly as much as I am Smith."

"Sir?" Jones gasped again.

Smith coughed discreetly. "But I have one advantage. I know you. You don't know me, Mr. Arkalion."

"Eh? Eh?"

"Arkalion. The North American Carpet King. Right?"

"How did you know?" the man whose name was not Jones but Arkalion asked the man whose name was not Smith but might as well have been.

"When I saw your ad," said not-Smith, "I said to myself, 'now here must be a very rich, influential man.' It only remained for me to study a series of photographs readily obtainable—I have a fine memory for that, Mr. Arkalion— and here you are; here is Arkalion the Carpet King."

"What will you do with the ten million dollars?" demanded Arkalion, not minding the loss nearly so much as the ultimate disposition of his fortune.

"Why, what does anyone do with ten minion dollars? Treasure it. Invest it. Spend it."

"I mean, what will you do with it if you are going in place of my—" Arkalion bit his tongue.

"Your son, were you saying, Mr. Arkalion? Alaric Arkalion the Third. Did you know that I was able to boil my list of men down to thirty when I studied their family ties?"

"Brilliant, Mr. Smith. Alaric is so young—"

"Aren't they all? Twenty-one to twenty-six. Who was it who once said something about the flower of our young manhood?"

"Shakespeare?" said Mr. Arkalion realizing that most quotes of lasting importance came from the bard.

"Sophocles," said Smith. "But, no matter. I will take young Alaric's place for ten million dollars."

Motives always troubled Mr. Arkalion, and thus he pursued what might have been a dangerous conversation. "You'll never get a chance to spend it on the Nowhere

Journey."

"Let me worry about that."

"No one ever returns."

"My worry, not yours."

"It is forever—as if you dropped out of existence. Alaric is so young."

"I have always gambled, Mr. Arkalion. If I do not return in five years, you are to put the money in a trust fund for certain designated individuals, said fund to be terminated the moment I return. If I come back within the five years, you are merely to give the money over to me. Is that clear?"

"Yes."

"I'll want it in writing, of course."

"Of course. A plastic surgeon is due here in about ten minutes, Mr. Smith, and we can get on with...but if I don't know your name, how can I put it in writing?"

Smith smiled. "I changed my name to Smith for the occasion. Perfectly legal. My name is John X. Smith—now."

"That's where you're wrong," said Mr. Arkalion as the plastic surgeon entered. "Your name is Alaric Arkalion III—now."

The plastic surgeon skittered around Smith, examining him minutely with the casual expertness that comes with experience.

"Have to shorten the cheek bones."

"For ten million dollars," said Smith, "you can take the damned things out altogether and hang them on your wall."

SOPHIA Androvna Petrovitch made her way downtown through the bustle of tired workers and the occasional sprinkling of Comrades. She crushed her ersatz cigarette underfoot at number 616 Stalin Avenue, paused for the space of five heartbeats at the door, went inside.

"What do you want?" The man at the desk was myopic but bullnecked.

Sophia showed her party card.

"Oh, Comrade. Still, you are a woman."

"You're terribly observant, Comrade," said Sophia coldly. "I am here to volunteer."

"But a woman."

"There is nothing in the law which says a woman cannot volunteer."

"We don't make women volunteer."

"I mean really volunteer, of her own free will."

"Her—own—free will?" The bull-necked man removed his spectacles, scratched his balding head with the earpieces. "You mean volunteer without—"

"Without coercion. I want to volunteer. I am here to volunteer. I want to sign on for the next Stalintrek."

"Stalintrek, a woman?"

"That is what I said."

"We don't force women to volunteer." The man scratched some more.

"Oh, really," said Sophia. "This is 1992, not mid-century, Comrade. Did not Premier Stalin say, Woman was created to share the glorious destiny of Mother Russia with her mate?'" Sophia created the quote randomly.

"Yes, if Stalin said—"

"He did."

"Still, I do not recall—"

"What?" Sophia cried. "Stalin dead these thirty-nine years and you don't recall his speeches? What is your name, Comrade?"

"Please, Comrade. Now that you remind me, I remember."

"What is your name."

"Here, I will give you the volunteer papers to sign. If you

pass the exams, you will embark on the next Stalintrek, though why a beautiful young woman like you—"

"Shut your mouth and hand me those papers."

There, sitting behind that desk, was precisely why. Why should she, Sophia Androvna Petrovitch, wish to volunteer for the Stalintrek? Better to ask why a bird flies south in the winter, one day ahead of the first icy gale. Or why a lemming plunges recklessly into the sea with his multitudes of fellows, if, indeed, the venture were to turn out grimly.

But there, behind that desk, was part of the reason. The Comrade. The bright sharp Comrade, with his depth of reasoning, his fountain of gushing emotions, his worldliness. *Pfooey!*

It was as if she had been in a cocoon all her life, stifled, starved, the cottony inner lining choking her whenever she opened her mouth, the leathery outer covering restricting her when she tried to move. None had ever returned from the Stalintrek. She then had to assume no one would. Including Sophia Androvna Petrovitch. But then, there was nothing she would miss, nothing to which she particularly wanted to return. Not the stark, foul streets of Stalingrad, not the workers with their vapid faces or the Comrades with their cautious, sweating, trembling, fearful non-decisions, not the higher echelon of Comrades, more frightened but showing it less, who would love the beauty of her breasts and loins but not herself for you never love anything but the Stalinimage and Mother Russia herself, not those terrified martinet-marionettes who would love the parts of her if she permitted, but not her or any other person for that matter.

Wrong with the Stalintrek was its name alone, a name one associated with everything else in Russia for an obvious, post-Stalin reason. But everything else about the Stalintrek shrieked mystery and adventure. Where did you go? How did you get there? What did you do? Why?

A million questions that had kept her awake at night and, if she thought about them hard enough, satisfied her deep longing for something different. And then one day when stolid Mrs. Ivanovna-Rasnikov had said, "It is a joke, a terrible, terrible joke they are taking my husband Fyodor on the Stalintrek when he lacks sufficient imagination to go from here to Leningrad or even Tula. Can you picture Fyodor on the Stalintrek? Better they should have taken me. Better they should have taken his wife." That day Sophia could hardly contain herself.

As a party member she had access to the law and she read it three times from start to finish (in her dingy flat by the light of a smoking, foul-smelling, soft-wax candle) but could find nothing barring women from the Stalintrek.

Had Fyodor Rasnikov volunteered? Naturally. Everyone volunteered, although when your name was called you had no choice. There had been no draft in Russia since the days of the Second War of the People's Liberation. Volunteer? What, precisely, did the word mean?

She, Sophia Androvna Petrovitch would volunteer, without being told. Thus it was she found herself at 616 Stalin Avenue, and thus the balding, myopic, bullnecked Comrade thrust the papers across his desk at her.

She signed her name with such vehemence and ferocity that she almost tore through the paper.

CHAPTER TWO

Three-score men sit in the crowded, smoke-filled room. Some drink beer, some squat in moody silence, some talk in an animated fashion about nothing very urgent. At the one small door, two guards pace back and forth slowly, creating a gentle swaying of smoke-patterns in the hazy room. The guards, in simple military uniform, carry small, deadly looking weapons.

FIRST MAN: Fight City Hall? Are you kidding? They took you, bud. Don't try to fight it. I know. I know.

SECOND MAN: I'm telling you, there was a mistake in the records. I'm over twenty-six. Two weeks and two days. Already I wrote to my Congressman. Hell, that's why I voted for him, he better go to bat for me.

THIRD MAN: You think that's something? I wouldn't be here only these doctors are crazy. I mean, crazy. Me, with a cyst big as a golf ball on the base of my spine.

FIRST MAN: You too. Don't try to fight it.

FOURTH MAN: (Newly named Alaric Arkalion III) I look forward to this as a stimulating adventure. Does the fact that they select men for the Nowhere Journey once every seven hundred and eighty days strike anyone as significant?

SECOND MAN: I got my own problems.

ALARIC ARKALION: This is not a thalamic problem, young man. Not thalamic at all.

THIRD MAN: Young man? Who are you kidding?

ALARIC ARKALION: (Who realizes, thanks to the plastic surgeon, he is the youngest looking of all, with red cheeks and peach fuzz whiskers) It is a problem of the intellect. Why seven hundred and eighty days?

FIRST MAN: I read the magazines, too, chief. You think

we're all going to the planet Mars. How original.

ALARIC ARKALION: As a matter of fact, that is exactly what I think.

SECOND MAN: Mars?

FIRST MAN (Laughing) It's a long way from Mars to City Hall, doc.

SECOND MAN: You mean, through space to Mars?

ALARIC ARKALION: Exactly, exactly. Quite a coincidence, otherwise.

FIRST MAN: You're telling me.

ALARIC ARKALION: (Coldly) Would you care to explain it?

FIRST MAN: Why, sure. You see, Mars is—uh, I don't want to steal your thunder, chief. Go ahead.

ALARIC ARKALION: Once every seven hundred and eighty days Mars and the Earth find themselves in the same orbital position with respect to the sun. In other words, Mars and Earth are closest then. Were there such, a thing as space travel, new, costly, not thoroughly tested, they would want to make each journey as brief as possible. Hence the seven hundred and eighty days.

FIRST MAN: Not bad, chief. You got most of it.

THIRD MAN: No one ever said anything about space travel.

FIRST MAN: You think we'd broadcast it or something, stupid? It's part of a big, important scientific experiment, only we're the hamsters.

ALARIC ARKALION: Ridiculous. You're forgetting all about the Cold War.

FIRST MAN: He thinks we're fighting a war with the Martians. (Laughs) Orson Welles stuff, huh?

ALARIC ARKALION: With the Russians. The Russians. We developed A bombs. They developed A bombs. We came up with the H-bomb. So did they. We placed a station up in space, a fifth of the way to the moon. So did they. Then—nothing more about scientific developments. For over twenty years. I ask you, doesn't it seem peculiar?

FIRST MAN: Peculiar, he says.

ALARIC ARKALION: Peculiar.

SECOND MAN: I wish my Congressman…

FIRST MAN: You and your Congressman. The way you talk, it was your vote got him in office.

SECOND MAN: If only I could get out and talk to him.

ALARIC ARKALION: No one is permitted to leave.

FIRST MAN: Punishable by a prison term, the law says.

SECOND MAN. Oh yeah? Prison, shmision. Or else go on the Nowhere Journey. Well, I don't see the difference.

FIRST MAN: So, go ahead. Try to escape.

SECOND MAN: (Looking at the guards) They got them all over. All over. I think our mail is censored.

ALARIC ARKALION: It is.

SECOND MAN: They better watch out. I'm losing my temper. I get violent when I lose my temper.

FIRST MAN: See? See how the guards are trembling.

SECOND MAN: Very funny. Maybe you didn't have a good job or something? Maybe you don't care. I care. I had a job with a future. Didn't pay much, but a real blue chip future. So they send me to Nowhere.

FIRST MAN: You're not there yet.

SECOND MAN: Yeah, but I'm going.

THIRD MAN: If only they let you know when. My back is killing me. I'm waiting to pull a sick act. Just waiting, that's all.

FIRST MAN: Go ahead and wait, a lot of good it will do you.

THIRD MAN: You mind your own business.

FIRST MAN: I am, doc. It was you who brought the whole thing up.

SECOND MAN; He's looking for trouble.

THIRD MAN: He'll get it.

ALARIC ARKALION: We're go ing to be together a long time. A long time. Why don't you all relax?

SECOND MAN: You mind your own business.

FIRST MAN: Nuts, aren't they. They're nuts. A sick act, yet.

SECOND MAN: Look how it doesn't bother him. A failure, he was. I can just see it. What does he care if he goes away forever and doesn't come back? One bread line is as good as another.

FIRST MAN: Ha-ha.

SECOND MAN: Yeah, well I mean it. Forever. We're going away, someplace—forever. We're not coming back, ever. No one comes back. It's for good, for keeps.

FIRST MAN: Tell it to your Congressman. Or maybe you want to pull a sick act, too?

THIRD MAN: (Hits First Man, who, surprised, crashes back against a table and falls down) It isn't an act, damn you!

GUARD: All right, break it up. Come on, break it up…

ALARIC ARKALION: (To himself) I wish I saw that, ten million dollars already—if I ever get to see it.

THEY drove for hours through the fresh country air, feeling the wind against their faces, listening to the roar their ground-jet made, all alone on the rimrock highway.

"Where are we going, Kit?"

"Search me. Just driving."

"I'm glad they let you come out this once. I don't know what they would have done to me if they didn't. I had to see you this once. I—"

Temple smiled. He had absented himself without leave. It had been difficult enough and he might yet be in a lot of hot water, but it would be senseless to worry Stephanie. "It's just for a few hours," he said.

"Hours. When we want a whole lifetime. Kit. Oh, Kit—why don't we run away? Just the two of us, someplace where they'll never find you. I could be packed and ready and—"

"Don't talk like that. We can't."

"You want to go where they're sending you. You want to go."

"For God's sake, how can you talk like that? I don't want to go anyplace, except with you. But we can't run away, Steffy. I've got to face it, whatever it is."

"No you don't. It's noble to be patriotic, sure. It always was. But this is different, Kit. They don't ask for part of your life. Not for two years, or three, or a gamble because maybe you won't ever come back. They ask for all of you, for the rest of your life, forever, and they don't even tell you why. Kit…don't go! We'll hide someplace and get married and—"

"And nothing." Temple stopped the ground-jet, climbed out, and opened the door for Stephanie. "Don't you see? There's no place to hide. Wherever you go, they'd look. You wouldn't want to spend the rest of your life running, Steffy. Not with me or anyone else."

"I would. I would!"

"Know what would happen after a few years'? We'd hate each other. You'd look at me and say 'I wouldn't be hiding like this, except for you. I'm young and—' "

"Kit, that's cruel! I would not."

"Yes, you would. Steffy, I—" A lump rose in his throat. He'd tell her goodbye, permanently. He had to do it that way, did not want her to wait endlessly and hopelessly for a return that would not materialize. "I didn't get permission to leave, Steffy." he hadn't meant to tell her that, but suddenly it seemed an easy way to break into goodbye.

"What do you mean? No—you didn't…"

"I had to see you. What can they do, send me for longer

than forever?"

"Then you do want to run away with me!"

"Steffy, no. When I leave you tonight, Steffy, it's for good. That's it. The last of Kit Temple. Stop thinking about me. I don't exist. I—never was." It sounded ridiculous, even to him.

"Kit, I love you. I love you. How can I forget you?"

"It's happened before. It will happen again." That hurt, too. He was talking about a couple of statistics, not about himself and Stephanie.

"We're different, Kit. I'll love you forever. And—Kit...I know you'll come back to me. I'll wait, Kit. We're different. You'll come back."

"How many people do you think said that before?"

"You don't want to come back, even if you could. You're not thinking of us at all. You're thinking of your brother."

"You know that isn't true. Sometimes I wonder about Jase, sure. But if I thought there was a chance to return—I'm a selfish cuss, Steffy. If I thought there was a chance, you know I'd want you all for myself. I'd brand you, and that's the truth."

"You do love me!"

"I loved you, Steffy. Kit Temple loved you."

"Loved?"

"Loved. Past tense. When I leave tonight, it's as if I don't exist anymore. As if I never existed. It's got to be that way, Steffy. In thirty years, no one ever returned."

"Including your brother, Jase. So now you want to find him. What do I count for? What..."

"This going wasn't my idea. I wanted to stay with" you. I wanted to marry you. I can't now. None of it. Forget me, Steffy. Forget you ever knew me. Jase said that to our folks before he was taken." Almost five years before Jason Temple had been selected for the Nowhere Journey. He'd been

young, though older than his brother Kit. Young, un-
attached, almost cheerful he was. Naturally, they never saw
him again.

"Hold me, Kit. I'm sorry…carrying on like this."

They had walked some distance from the ground-jet,
through scrub oak and bramble bushes. They found a
clearing, fragrant-scented, soft-floored still from last autumn,
melodic with the chirping of nameless birds. They sat, not
talking. Stephanie wore a gay summer dress, full-skirted, cut
deep beneath the throat. She swayed toward him from the
waist, nestled her head on his shoulder. He could smell the
soft, sweet fragrance of her hair, of the skin at the nape of her
neck. "If you want to say goodbye…" she said.

"Stop it," he told her.

"If you want to say goodbye…"

Her head rolled against his chest. She turned, cradled
herself in his arms, smiled up at him, squirmed some more
and had her head pillowed on his lap. She smiled
tremulously, misty-eyed. Her lips parted.

He bent and kissed her, knowing it was all wrong. This
was not goodbye, not the way he wanted it. Quickly,
definitely, for once and all. With a tear, perhaps, a lot of
tears. But permanent goodbye. This was all wrong. The
whole idea was to be business-like, objective. It had to be
done that way, or no way at all. Briefly, he regretted leaving
the encampment.

This wasn't goodbye the way he wanted it. The way it had
to be. This was auf weidersen.

And then he forgot everything but Stephanie…

"I AM Alaric Arkalion, III," said the extremely young--
looking man with the old, wise eyes.

How incongruous, Temple thought. The eyes look almost
middle-aged. The rest of him—a boy.

"Something tells me we'll be seeing a lot of each other," Arkalion went on. The voice was that of an older man, too, belying the youthful complexion, the almost childish features, the soft fuzz of a beard.

"I'm Kit Temple," said Temple, extending his hand. "Arkalion, a strange name. I know it from somewhere... Say! Aren't you—don't you have something to do with carpets or something?"

"Here and now, no. I am a number. A-92-6417. But my father is—perhaps I had better say was—my father is Alaric Arkalion II. Yes, that is right, the carpet king."

"I'll be darned," said Temple.

"Why?"

"Well," Temple laughed. "I never met a billionaire before."

"Here I am not a billionaire, nor will I ever be one again. A-92-6417, a number. On his way to Mars with a bunch of other numbers."

"Mars? You sound sure of yourself."

"Reasonably. Ah, it is a pleasure to talk with a gentleman. I am reasonably certain it will be Mars."

Temple nodded in agreement. "That's what the Sunday supplements say, all right."

"And doubtless you have observed no one denies it."

"But what on Earth do we want on Mars?"

"That in itself is a contradiction," laughed Arkalion. "We'll find out, though, Temple."

They had reached the head of the line, found themselves entering a huge, double-decker jet-transport. They found two seats together, followed the instructions printed at the head of the aisle by strapping themselves in and not smoking. Talking all around them was subdued.

"Contrariness has given way to fear," Arkalion observed. "You should have seen them the last few days, waiting around the induction center, a two-ton chip on each shoulder. Say, where were you?"

"I—what do you mean?"

"I didn't see you until last evening. Suddenly, you were here."

"Did anyone else miss me?"

"But I remember you the first day."

"Did anyone else miss me? Any of the officials?"

"No. Not that I know of."

"Then I was here," Temple said, very seriously.

Arkalion smiled. "By George, of course. Then you were here. Temple, we'll get along fine."

Temple said that was swell.

"Anyway, we'd better. Forever is a long time."

Three minutes later, the jet took off and soared on eager wings toward the setting sun.

"MEN, since we are leaving here in a few hours and since there is no way to get out of the encampment and no place to go over the desert even if you could," the microphone in the great, empty hall boomed as the two files of men marched in, "there is no harm in telling you where you are. From this point, in a limited sense, you shall be kept abreast of your progress.

"We are in White Sands, New Mexico."

"The Garden Spot of the Universe!" someone shouted derisively, remembering the bleak hot desert and jagged mountain peaks as they came down.

"White Sands," muttered Arkalion. "It looks like space travel now, doesn't it, Kit."

Temple shrugged. "Why?"

"White sands was the center of experiments in rocketry decades ago, when people still talked about those things. Then, for a long time, no one heard anything about White

Sands. The rockets grew here, Kit."

"I can readily see why. You could look all your life without finding a barren spot like this."

"Precisely. Someone once called this place—or was it some other place like it?—someone once called it a good place to throw old razorblades. If people still used razor blades."

The microphone blared again, after the several hundred men had entered the great hall and milled about among the echoes. Temple could picture other halls like this, other briefings. "Men, whenever you are given instructions, in here or elsewhere, obey them instantly. Our job is a big one, complicated and exacting. Attention to detail will save us trouble."

Someone said, "My old man served a hitch in the army, back in the sixties. That's what he always said, attention to details. The army is crazy about things like that. Are we in the army or something?"

"This is not the army, but the function is similar," barked the microphone. "Do as you are told and you will get along."

Stirrings in the crowd. Mutterings. Temple gaped. Microphone, yes—but receivers also, placed strategically, all around the hall, to pick up sound. Telio receivers too, perhaps? It made him feel something like a goldfish.

Apparently someone liked the idea or the two-way microphones. "I got a question. When are we coming back?"

Laughter. Hooting. Catcalls.

Blared the microphone: "There is a rotation system in operation, men. When it is feasible, men will be rotated."

"Yeah, in thirty years it ain't been whatsiz—feasible—once!"

"That, unfortunately, is correct. When the situation permits, we will rotate you home."

"From where? Where are we going?"

"At least tell us that."

"Where?"

"How about that?"

There was a pause, then the microphone barked: "I don't know the answer to that question. You won't believe me, but it is the truth. No one knows where you are going. No one. Except the people who are already there."

More catcalls.

"That doesn't make sense," Arkalion whispered. "If it's space travel, the pilots would know, wouldn't they?"

"Automatic?" Temple suggested. "I doubt it. Space travel must still be new, even if it has thirty years under its belt. If that man speaks the truth...if no one knows...then just where in the universe are we going?"

CHAPTER THREE

"HEY, looka' me. I'm flying!"

"Will you get your big fat feet out of my face?"

"Sure. Show me how to swim away through air, I'll be glad to."

"Leggo that spoon!"

"I ain't got your spoon."

"Will you look at it float away. Hey spoon, hey!"

"Watch this, Charlie. This will get you. I mean, get you."

"What are you gonna do?"

"Relax, chum."

"Leggo my leg. Help! I'm up in the air. Stop that."

"I said relax. There. Ha-ha, lookit him spin, just like a top. All you got to do is get him started and he spins like a top with arms and legs. Top of the morning to you, Charlie. Ha-ha, I said, top of the..."

"Someone stop me. I'm getting dizzy."

They floated, tumbled, spun around the spaceship's lounge room in simple, childish glee. They cavorted in festive weightlessness.

"They're happy now," Arkalion observed. "The novelty of free fall, of weighing exactly nothing, strikes them as amusing."

"I think I'm getting the hang of it," said Temple. Clumsily, he made a few tentative swimming motions in the air, propelling himself forward a few yards before he lost his balance and tumbled head over heels against the wall.

Arkalion came to him quickly, in a combination of swimming and pushing with hands and feet against the wall. Arkalion righted him expertly, sat down gingerly beside him.

"If you keep sudden motions to a minimum, you'll get along fine. More than anything else, that's the secret of it."

Temple nodded. "It's sort of like the first time you're on ice skates. Say, how come you're so good at it?"

"I used to read the old, theoretical books on space-travel." The words poured out effortlessly, smoothly. "I'm merely applying the theories put forward as early as the 1950's."

"Oh." But it left Temple with some food for thought. Alaric Arkalion was a queer duck, anyway, and of all the men gathered in the spaceship's lounge, he alone had mastered weightlessness with hardly any trouble.

"Take your ice skates," Arkalion went on. "Some people put them on and use them like natural extensions of their feet the first time. Others fall all over themselves. I suppose I am lucky."

"Sure," said Temple. Actually, the only thing odd about Arkalion was his old-young face and—perhaps—his propensity for coming up with the right answers at the right times. Arkalion had seemed so certain of space-travel. He'd hardly batted an eyelash when they boarded a long, tapering, bullet-shaped ship at White Sands and thundered off into the sky. He took for granted the changeover to a huge round ship at the wheel-shaped station in space. Moments after leaving the space station—with a minimum of stress and strain, thanks to the almost-nil gravity—it was Arkalion who first swam through air to the viewport and pointed out the huge crescent earth, green and gray and brown, sparkling with patches of dazzling silver-white. "You will observe it is a crescent," Arkalion had said. "It is closer to the sun than we are, and off at an angle. As I suspected, our destination is Mars."

THEN everyone was saying goodbye to earth. Fantastic, it truly seemed. There were tears, there was laughter, cursing,

promises of return, awkward verbal comparisons with the crescent moon, vows of faithfulness to lovers and sweethearts. And there was Arkalion, with an avid expression in the old eyes; Arkalion with his boyish face, not saying goodbye so much as he was calling hello to something Temple could not fathom.

Now, as he struggled awkwardly with weightlessness, Temple called it his imagination. His thought patterns shifted vaguely, without motivation, from the gleaming, polished interior of the ship with its smell of antiseptic and metal polish to the clear Spring air of Earth, blue of sky and bright of sun. The unique blue sky of Earth, which he somehow knew could not be duplicated elsewhere. Elsewhere—the word itself bordered on the meaningless.

And Stephanie. The brief warm ecstasy of her—once, forever. He wondered with surprising objectivity if a hundred other names, a hundred other women were not in a hundred other minds while everyone stared at the crescent Earth hanging serenely in space—with each name and each woman as dear as Stephanie, with the same combination of fire and gentle femininity stirring the blood but saddening the heart. Would Stephanie really forget him? Did he want her to? That part of him burned by the fire of her said no—no, she must not forget him. She was his, his alone, roped and branded though a universe separated them. But someplace in his heart was the thought, the understanding, the realization that although Stephanie might keep a small place for him tucked someplace deep in her emotions, she must forget. He was gone—permanently. For Stephanie, he was dead. It was as he had told her that last stolen day. It was...*Stephanie, Stephanie, how much I love you...*

Struggling with weightlessness, he made his way back to the small room he shared with Arkalion. Hardly more than a cubicle, it was, with sufficient room for two beds, a sink, a small chest. He lay down and slept, murmuring Stephanie's name in his sleep.

HE awoke to the faint hum of the air-pumps, got up

feeling rested, forgot his weightlessness and floated to the ceiling where only an out thrust arm prevented a nasty bump on his head. He used handgrips on the wall to let himself down. He washed, aware of no way to prevent the water he splashed on his face from forming fine droplets and spraying the entire room. When he crossed back to the foot of his bed to get his towel he thrust one foot out too rapidly, lost his balance, half-rose, stumbled and fell against the other bed which, like all other items of furniture, was fastened to the floor. But his elbow struck sleeping Arkalion's jaw sharply, hard enough to jar the man's teeth.

"I'm sorry," said Temple. "Didn't mean to do that," he apologized again, feeling embarrassed.

Arkalion merely lay there.

"I said I'm sorry."

Arkalion still slept. It seemed inconceivable, for Temple's elbow pained him considerably. He bent down and examined his inert companion.

Arkalion stirred not a muscle.

Vaguely alarmed, Temple thrust a hand to Arkalion's chest, felt nothing. He crouched, rested the side of his head over Arkalion's heart. He listened, heard—nothing.

What was going on here?

"Hey, Arkalion!" Temple shook him, gently at first, then with savage force. Weightless, Arkalion's body floated up off the bed, taking the covers with it. His own heart pounding furiously, Temple got it down again, fingered the left wrist and swallowed nervously.

Temple had never seen a dead man before. Arkalion's heart did not beat. Arkalion had no pulse.

Arkalion was dead.

Yelling hoarsely, Temple plunged from the room, soaring off the floor in his haste and striking his head against the ceiling hard enough to make him see stars. "This guy is dead!" he cried. "Arkalion is dead."

Men stirred in the companionway. Someone called for one of the armed guards who were constantly on patrol.

"If he's dead, you're yelling loud enough to get him out of his grave." The voice was quiet, amused.

Arkalion.

"What?" Temple blurted, whirling around and striking his head again. A little wild-eyed, he reentered the room.

"Now, who is dead, Kit?" demanded Arkalion, sitting up and stretching comfortably.

"Who—is dead? Who—?" Open-mouthed, Temple stared.

A GUARD, completely at home with weightlessness, entered the cubicle briskly. "What's the trouble in here? Something about a dead man, they said."

"A dead man?" demanded Arkalion. "Indeed."

"Dead?" muttered Temple, lamely and foolishly. "Dead…"

Arkalion smiled deprecatingly. "My friend must have been talking in his sleep. The only thing dead in here is my appetite. Weightlessness doesn't let you become very hungry."

"You'll grow used to it," the guard promised. He patted his paunch happily. "I am. Well, don't raise the alarm unless there's some trouble. Remember about the boy who cried wolf."

"Of course," said Temple. "Sure. Sorry."

He watched the guard depart. "Bad dream?" Arkalion wanted to know.

"Bad dream, my foot. I accidentally hit you. Hard enough to hurt. You didn't move."

"I'm a sound sleeper."

"I felt for your heart. It wasn't beating. It wasn't!"

"Oh, come, come."

"Your heart was not beating, I said."

"And I suppose I was cold as a slab of ice?"

"Umm, no. I don't remember. Maybe you were. You had no pulse, either."

Arkalion laughed easily. "And am I still dead?"

"Well—"

"Clearly a case of overwrought nerves and a highly keyed imagination. What you need is some more sleep."

"I'm not sleepy, thanks."

"Well, I think I'll get up and go down for breakfast." Arkalion climbed out of bed gingerly, made his way to the sink and was soon gargling with a bottle of prepared mouthwash, occasionally spraying weightless droplets of the pink liquid up at the ceiling.

Temple lit a cigarette with shaking fingers, made his way to Arkalion's bed while the man hummed tunelessly at the sink. Temple let his hands fall on the sheet. It was not cold, but comfortably cool. Hardly as warm as it should have been, with a man sleeping on it all night.

Was he still imagining things? "I'm glad you didn't call for a burial detail and have me expelled into space with yesterday's garbage," Arkalion called over his shoulder jauntily as he went outside for some breakfast.

Temple cursed softly and lit another cigarette, dropping the first one into a disposal chute on the wall.

EVERY night thereafter, Temple made it a point to remain awake after Arkalion apparently had fallen asleep. But if he were seeking repetition of the peculiar occurrence, he was disappointed. Not only did Arkalion sleep soundly and through the night, but he snored. Loudly and clearly, a wheezing snore.

Arkalion's strange feat—or his own overwrought

imagination, Temple thought wryly—was good for one thing: it took his mind off Stephanie. The days wore on in endless, monotonous routine. He took some books from the ship's library and browsed through them, even managing to find one concerned with traumatic catalepsy, which stated that a severe emotional shock might render one into a deep enough trance to have a layman mistakenly pronounce him dead. But what had been the severe emotional disturbance for Arkalion? Could the effects of weightlessness manifest themselves in that way in rare instances? Temple naturally did not know, but he resolved to find out if he could after reaching their destination.

One day—it was three weeks after they left the space station, Temple realized—they were all called to assembly in the ship's large main lounge. As the men drifted in, Temple was amazed to see the progress they had made with weightlessness. He himself had advanced to handy facility in locomotion, but it struck him all the more pointedly when he saw two hundred men swim and float through air, pushing themselves along by means of the handholds strategically placed along the walls.

The ever-present microphone greeted them all. "Good afternoon, men."

"Good afternoon, Mac!"

"Hey, is this the way to Ebbetts' Field?"

"Get on with it!"

"Sounds like the same man who addressed us in White Sands," Temple told Arkalion. "He sure does get around."

"A recording, probably. Listen."

"Our destination, as you've probably read in newspapers and magazines, is the planet Mars."

Mutterings in the assembly, not many of surprise.

"Their suppositions, based both on the seven hundred eighty day lapse between Nowhere Journeys and the romantic position in which the planet Mars has always been held, are correct. We are going to Mars.

"For most of you, Mars will be a permanent home for many years to come—"

"Most of us?" Temple wondered out loud.

Arkalion raised a finger to his lips for silence.

"—until such time as you are rotated according to the policy of rotation set up by the government."

Temple had grown accustomed to the familiar hoots and catcalls. He almost had an urge to join in himself.

"Interesting," Arkalion pointed out. "Back at White Sands they claimed not to know our destination. They knew it all right up to a point. The planet Mars. But now they say that all of us will not remain on Mars. Most interesting."

"—further indoctrination in our mission soon after our arrival on the red planet. Landing will be performed under somewhat less strain than the initial takeoff in the Earth-to-station ferry, since Mars exerts less of a gravity pull than Earth. On the other hand, you have been weightless for three weeks and the changeover is liable to make some of you sick. It will pass harmlessly enough.

"We realize it is difficult, being taken from your homes without knowing the nature of your urgent mission. All I can tell you now—and, as a matter of fact, all I know—"

"Here we go again," said Temple. "More riddles."

"—is that everything is of the utmost urgency. Our entire way of life is at stake. Our job will be to safeguard it. In the months that follow, few of you will have any big, significant roles to play, but all of you, working together, will provide the strength we need. When the *cadre*—"

"So they call their guards teachers," Arkalion commented dryly.

"—come around, they will see that each man is strapped properly into his bunk for deceleration. Deceleration begins in twenty-seven minutes."

Mars, thought Temple, back in his room with Arkalion. Mars. He did not think of Stephanie, except as a man who knows he must spend the rest of his life in prison might think of a lush green field, or the cool swish of skis over fresh, powdery snow, or the sound of yardarms creaking against the wind on a small sailing schooner, or the tang of wieners roasting over an open fire with the crisp air of fall against your back, or the scent of good French brandy, or a woman.

Deceleration began promptly. Before his face was distorted and his eyes forced shut by a pressure of four gravities, Temple had time to see the look of complete unconcern on Arkalion's face. Arkalion, in fact, was sleeping.

He seemed as completely relaxed as he did that morning Temple thought he was dead.

CHAPTER FOUR

"PETROVITCH, S. A.!" caned the Comrade standing abreast of the head of the line, a thin, nervous man half a head shorter than the girl herself. Sophia Androvna Petrovitch strode forward, took a pair of trim white shorts from the neat stack at his left.

"Is that all?" she said, looking at him.

"Yes, Comrade. Well, a woman. Well."

Without embarrassment, Sophia had seen the men ahead of her in line strip and climb into the white shorts before they disappeared through a portal ahead of the line, depositing their clothing in a growing pile on the floor. But now it was Sophia's turn, after almost a two-hour wait. Not that it was chilly, but...

"Is that all?" she repeated.

"Certainly. Strip and move along, Comrade." The nervous little man appraised her lecherously, she thought.

"Then I must keep some of my own clothing," she told him.

"Impossible. I have my orders."

"I am a woman."

"You are a volunteer for the Stalintrek. You will take no personal property—no clothing—with you. Strip and advance, please."

Sophia flushed slightly, while the men behind her began to call and taunt.

"I like this Stalintrek."

"Oh, yes."

"We are waiting, Comrade."

Quickly and with an objective detachment that surprised

122

her, Sophia unbuttoned her shirt, removed it. Her one wish—and an odd one, she thought, smiling—was for the wax for her ears. She loosened the three snaps of her skirt, watched it fall to the floor. She stood there briefly, lithe-limbed, a tall, slim girl, then had the white shorts over her nakedness in one quick motion. She still wore a coarse halter.

"All personal effects, Comrade," said the nervous little man.

"No," Sophia told him.

"But yes. Definitely, yes. You hold up the line, and we have a schedule to maintain. The Stalintrek demands quick, prompt obedience."

"The you will give me one additional item of clothing."

The man looked at Sophia's halter, at the fine way she filled it. He shrugged. "We don't have it," he said, clearly enjoying himself.

In volunteering for the Stalintrek, Sophia had invaded man's domain. She had watched not with embarrassment but with scorn while the men in front of her got out of their clothing. She had invaded man's domain, and as she watched them, the short, flabby ones, the bony ones with protruding ribs and collar-bones, those of milky white skin and soft hands, she knew most of them would bite off more than they could chew if ever they tried what was the most natural thing for men to try with a lone woman in an isolated environment. But she *was* in a man's world now, and if that was the way they wanted it, she would ask no quarter.

She reached up quickly with one hand and unfastened the halter, catching it with her free hand and holding it in front of her breasts while the nervous little man licked his lips and gaped. Sophia grabbed another pair of the white shorts, tore it quickly with her strong fingers, fashioning a crude covering for herself. This she pulled around her, fastening it securely with a knot in back.

"You'll have to give that back to me," declared the nervous little Comrade.

"I'll bet you a samovar on that," Sophia said quietly, so only the man heard her.

He reached out, as if to rip the crude halter from her body, but Sophia met him halfway with her strong, slim fingers, wrapping them around his biceps and squeezing. The man's face turned quickly to white as he tried unsuccessful to free his arm.

"Please, that hurts."

"I keep what I am wearing." She tightened her grip, but gazed serenely into space as the man stifled a whimper.

"Well—" the man whispered indecisively as he gritted his teeth.

"Fool!" said Sophia. "Your arm will be black and blue for a week. While you men grow soft and lazy, many of the women take their gymnastics seriously, especially if they want to keep their figures with the work they must do and the food they must eat. I am stronger than you and I will hurt you un- less—" And her hand tightened around his scrawny arm until her knuckles showed white.

"Wear what you have and go," the man pleaded, and moaned softly when Sophia released his numb arm and strode through the portal, still drawing whistles and leers from the other men, who missed the by-play completely.

"SO we're on Mars!"

"It ain't nowhere after all, it's Mars."

"Wait and see, buster. Wait and see."

"Kind of cold, isn't it? Well, if this was Venus and some of them beautiful one-armed dames was waiting for us—"

"That's just a statue, stupid."

"Lookit all them people down there, will you?"

"You think they're Martians?"

"Stupid! We ain't the first ones went on the Nowhere Journey."

"What are we waiting for? It sure will feel good to stretch your legs."

"Let's go!"

"Look out, Mars, here I come!"

It would have been just right for a Hollywood epic, Temple thought. The rusty ochre emptiness spreading out toward the horizon in all directions, spotted occasionally with pale green and frosty white, the sky gray with but a shade of blue in it, distant gusts of Martian wind swirling ochre clouds across the desert, the spaceship poised on its ungainly bottom, a great silver bowling ball with rocket tubes for finger holes, and the Martians from Earth who had been here on this alien world for seven-hundred-eighty days or twice seven-eighty or three times, and who fought in frenzied eagerness, like savages, to reach the descending gangplank first.

Earth chorus: Hey, Martians, any of you guys speak English? Ha-ha, I said, any of you guys...

Where are all them canals I heard so much about?

You think maybe they're dangerous? (Laughter)

No dames. Hey, no dames...

Who were you expecting, Donna Daunley?

What kind of place is Mars with no women?

What do they do here, anyway, just sit around and wait for the next rocket?

I'm cold.

Get used to it, brother, get used to it.

Look out, Mars, here I come!

Martian chorus: Who won the Series last year, Detroit?

Hey, bud, tell me, are dames still wearing those one-piece things, all colors, so you see their legs up to about here and their chests down to about here? (Gestures lewdly)

Which one of you guys can tell me what it's like to take a bath? I mean a real bath in a real bathtub.

Hey, we licked Russia yet?

We heard they were gonna send some dames!

Dames—ha-ha, you're breaking my heart.

Tell me what a steak tastes like. So thick.

Me? Gimme a bowl of steamed oysters and a dame.

Dames. Girls. Women. Females. Chicks. Tomatoes. Frails. Dames. Dames. Dames...

They did not seem to mind the cold, these Earth-Martians. Temple guessed they never spent much time out of doors (above ground, for there were no buildings?) because all seemed pale and white. While the sun was weaker, so was the protection offered by a thinner atmosphere. The sun's actinic rays could, burn, and so could the sand-driving wind. But pale skins could not be the result of staying indoors, for Temple noted the lack of man-made structures at once. Underground, then. The Earth-Martians lived underground like moles. Doing what? And for what reason? With what ultimate goal, if any? And where did those men who did not remain on Mars go? Temple's head whirled with countless questions—and no answers.

Shoulder to shoulder with Arkalion, he made his way down the gangplank, turning up the collar of his jumper against the stinging wind.

"You got any newspapers, pal?"

"Magazines?"

"Phonograph records?"

"Gossip?"

"News film?"

"Who's the heavyweight champ?"

"We lick those Commies in Burma yet?"

"Step back! Watch that man. Maybe he's your replacement."

"Replacement. Ha-ha. That's good."

All types of men. All ages. In torn, tattered clothing, mostly. In rags. Even if a man seemed more well-groomed than the rest, on closer examination Temple could see the careful stitching, the patches, the fades and stains. No one seemed to mind.

"Hey, bud. What do you hear about rotation? They passed any laws yet?"

"I been here ten years. When do I get rotated?"

"Ain't that something? Dad Jenks came here with the first ship. Don't you talk about rotation. Ask Dad."

"Better not mention that word to Dad Jenks. He sees red."

"This whole damn planet is red."

"Want a guided tour of nowhere, men? Step right up."

Arkalion grinned. "They seem so well-adjusted," he said, then shuddered against the cold and followed Temple, with the others, through the crowd.

THEY were inoculated against nameless diseases, (Watch for the needle with the hook)

They were told again they had arrived on the planet Mars. (No kidding?)

Led to a drab underground city, dimly lit, dank, noisome with mold and mildew. (Quick, the chlorophyll)

Assigned bunks in a dormitory, with four men to a room. (Be it ever so humble—bah!)

Told to keep things clean and assigned temporarily to a garbage pickup detail. (For this I left Sheboygan?)

Read to from the Declaration of Independence, the Constitution and Public Law 1182 (concerned with the Nowhere Journey, it told them nothing they did not already know).

Given as complete a battery of tests, mental, emotional

and physical, as Temple ever knew existed. (Cripes, man! How the hell should I know what the cube root of 5 is? I never finished high school!)

Subjected to an exhaustive, overlong, and at times meaningless personal interview. (No, doc, honest. I never knew I had a—uh—anxiety neurosis. Is it dangerous?)

"How do you do, Temple? Sit down."

"Thank you."

"Thought you'd like to know that while your overall test score is not uncanny, it's decidedly high."

"So what?"

"So nothing—not necessarily. Except that with it you have a very well balanced personality. We can use you, Temple."

"That's why I'm here."

"I mean—elsewhere. Mars is only a way station, a training center for a select few. It takes an awful lot of administrative work to keep this place going, which explains the need for all the station personnel."

"Listen. The last few weeks I had everything thrown at me. Everything, the works. Mind answering one question?"

"Shoot."

"What's this all about?"

"Temple, I don't know!"

"You what?"

"I know you find it hard to believe, but I don't. There isn't a man here on Mars who knows the whole story, either—and certainly not on Earth. We know enough to keep everything in operation. And we know it's important, all of it, everything we do."

"You mentioned a need for some men elsewhere. Where?"

The psychiatrist shrugged. "I don't know. Somewhere. Anywhere." he spread his hands out eloquently. "That's where the Nowhere Journey comes in."

"Surely you can tell me something more than—"

"Absolutely not. It isn't that I don't want to. I can't. I don't know."

"Well, one more question I'd like you to answer."

The psychiatrist lit a cigarette, grinned. "Say, who is interviewing whom?"

"This one I think you can tackle. I have a brother, Jason Temple. Embarked on the Nowhere Journey five years ago. I wonder—"

"So that's the one factor in your psychograph we couldn't figure out—anxiety over your brother."

"I doubt it," shrugged Temple. "More likely my fiancée."

"Umm, common enough. You were to be married?"

"Yes." *Stephanie, what are you doing now? Right now?*

"That's what hurts the most... Well, yes, I can find out about your brother." The psychiatrist flicked a toggle on his desk. "Jamison, find what you can on Temple, Jason, year of—"

"1987," Temple supplied.

"1987. We'll wait."

After a moment or two, the voice came through, faintly metallic: "Temple, Jason. Arrival: 1987. Psychograph, 115b12. Mental aggregate, 98. Physcom, good to excellent. Training: two years, space perception concentrate, others. Shipped out: 1989."

So Jase had shipped out for—Nowhere.

"Someday you'll follow in your brother's footsteps, Temple. Now, though, I have a few hundred questions I'd like you to answer."

The psychiatrist hadn't exaggerated. Several hours of questioning followed. Once reminded of her, Temple found it hard to keep his thought off Stephanie.

He left the psychiatrist's office more confused than ever.

"GOOD morning, child. You are Stephanie Andrews?"

Stephanie hadn't felt up to working that first morning after Kit's final goodbye. She answered the door in her bathrobe, saw a small, middle-aged woman with graying hair and a kind face. "That's right. Won't you come in?"

"Thank you. I represent the Complete Emancipation League, Miss Andrews."

"Complete Emancipation League? Oh, something to do with politics. Really, I'm not much interested in—"

"That's entirely the trouble," declared the older woman. "Too many of us are not interested in politics. I'd like to discuss the C.E.L. with you, my dear, if you will bear with me a few minutes."

"All right," said Stephanie.

"Would you like a glass of sherry?"

"In the morning?" the older woman smiled.

"I'm sorry. Don't mind me. My fiancé left yesterday, took his final goodbye. He—he embarked on the Nowhere Journey."

"I realize that. It is precisely why I am here. My dear, the C.E.L. does not want to fight the government. If the government decides that the Nowhere Journey is vital for the welfare of the country—even if the government won't or can't explain what the Nowhere Journey is—that's all right with us. But if the government says there is a rotation system but does absolutely nothing about it, we're interested in that. Do you follow me?"

"Yes!" cried Stephanie. "Oh, yes. Go on."

"The C.E.L. has sixty-eight people in Congress for the current term. We hope to raise that number to seventy-five for next election. It's a long fight, a slow uphill fight, and frankly, my dear, we need all the help we can get. People— young women like yourself, my dear—are entirely too lethargic, if you'll forgive me."

"You ought to forgive me," said Stephanie, "if you will. You know, it's funny. I had vague ideas—about helping Kit, about finding some way to get him back. Only to tackle something like that alone...I'm only twenty-one, just a girl, and I don't know anyone important. No one ever comes back, that's what you hear. But there's a rotation system, you also hear that. If I can be of any help..."

"You certainly can, my dear. We'd be delighted to have you."

"Then, eventually, maybe, just maybe, we'll start getting them rotated home?"

"We can't promise a thing. We can only try. And I never did say we'd try to get the boys rotated, my dear. There is a rotation system in the law, right there in Public Law 1182. But if no men have ever been rotated, there must be a reason for it."

"Yes, but—"

"But we'll see. If for some reason rotation simply is not practicable, we'll find another way. Which is why we call ourselves the C.E.L.—Complete Emancipation League—for women. If men must embark on the Nowhere Journey—the least they can do is let their women volunteer to go along with them if they want to—since it may be forever. Let a bunch of women get to this Nowhere place and you'll never know what might happen, that's what I say."

Something about the gray haired woman's earthy confidence imbued Stephanie with an optimism she never expected. "Well," she said, smiling, "if we can't bring ourselves to Mohammed... No, that's all wrong! ...to the mountain...?"

"Yes, there's an old saying. But it isn't important. You get the idea. My dear, how would you like to go to Nowhere?"

"I—to Kit, anywhere, anywhere!" *I'll never forget yesterday,*

Kit darling. Never!

"I make no promises, Stephanie, but it may be sooner than you think. Morning be hanged, perhaps I will have some sherry after all. Umm, you wouldn't by any chance have some Canadian instead?"

Humming, Stephanie dashed into the kitchen for some glasses.

THERE were times when the real Alaric Arkalion III wished his father would mind his own business. Like that thing about the Nowhere Journey, for instance. Maybe Alaric Sr. didn't realize it, but being the spoiled son of a billionaire wasn't all fun. "I'm a dilettante," Alaric would tell himself often, gazing in the mirror, "a bored dilettante at the age of twenty-one."

Which in itself, he had to admit, wasn't too bad. But having reneged on the Nowhere Journey in favor of a stranger twice his age who now carried his, Alaric's face, had engendered some annoying complications. "You'll either have to hide or change your own appearance and identity, Alaric."

"Hide? For how long, father?"

"I can't be sure. Years, probably."

"That's crazy. I'm not going to hide for years."

"Then change your appearance. Your way of life. Your occupation."

"I have no occupation."

"Get one. Change your face, too. Your fingerprints. It can be done. Become a new man, live a new life."

In hiding there was boredom, impossible boredom. In the other alternative there was adventure, intrigue—but uncertainty. One part of young Alaric craved that uncertainty, the rest of him shunned it. In a way it was like the Nowhere Journey all over again.

"Maybe Nowhere wouldn't have been so bad," said Alaric to his father, choosing as a temporary alternative and retreat what he knew couldn't possibly happen.

Couldn't it?

"If I choose another identity, I'd be eligible again for the Nowhere Journey."

"By George, I hadn't considered that. No, wait. You could be older than twenty-six."

"I like it the way I am," Alaric said, pouting.

"Then you'll have to hide. I spent ten million dollars to secure your future, Alaric. I don't want you to throw it away."

Alaric pouted some more. "Let me think about it."

"Fair enough, but I'll want your answer tomorrow. Meanwhile, you are not to leave the house."

Alaric agreed verbally, but took the first opportunity that presented itself—that very night—to sneak out the servants' door, go downtown, and get stewed to the gills.

At two in the morning he was picked up by the police for disorderly conduct (it had happened before) after losing a fistfight to a much poorer, much meaner drunk in a downtown bar. They questioned Alaric at the police station, examined his belongings, went through his wallet, notified his home.

Fuming, Alaric Sr. rushed to the police station to get his son. He was met by the desk sergeant, a fat, balding man who wore his uniform in a slovenly fashion.

"Mr. Arkalion?" demanded the sergeant, picking at his teeth with a toothpick.

"Yes. I have come for Alaric, my son."

"Sure. Sure. But your son's in trouble, Mr. Arkalion, Serious trouble."

"What are you talking about? If there are any damages, I'll pay. He didn't—hurt anyone, did he?"

The sergeant broke the toothpick between his teeth, laughed. "Him? Naw. He got the hell beat out of him by a drunk half his size. It ain't that kind of trouble, Mr. Arkalion. You know what an 1182 card is, mister?"

Arkalion's face drained white. "Why—yes."

"Alaric's got one."

"Naturally."

"According to the card, he should have shipped out on the Nowhere Journey, mister. He didn't. He's in serious trouble."

"I'll see the district attorney."

"More'n likely, you'll see the attorney general. Serious trouble."

CHAPTER FIVE

THE trouble with the Stalintrek, Sophia thought, was that it took months to get absolutely nowhere. There had been the painful pressure, the loss of consciousness, the confinement in this tight little world of dormitories and gleaming metal walls, the uncanny feeling of no weight, the ability—boring after a while, but interesting at first—to float about in air almost at will.

Then, how many months of sameness? Sophia had lost all track of time through *ennui*. But for the first brief period of adjustment on the part of her fellows to the fact that although she was a woman and shared their man's life she was still to be inviolate, the routine had been anything but exciting. The period of adjustment had had its adventures, its uncertain ties, its challenge, and to Sophia it had been stimulating. Why was it, she wondered, that the men who carried their sex with strength and dignity, the hard-muscled men who could have their way with her if they resorted to force were the men who did not violate her privacy, while the weaklings, the softer, smaller men, or the average men whom Sophia considered her physical equals were the ones who gave her trouble?

She had always accepted her beauty, the obvious attraction men found in her, with an objective unconcern. She had been endowed with sex appeal; there was not much room in her life to exploit it, even had she wanted to. Now, now when she wanted anything but that, it gave her trouble.

Her room was shared, of necessity, with three men. Tall, gangling Boris gave her no trouble, turned his back when she undressed for the evening, even though she was careful to slip under the covers first. Ivan, the second man, was short, thin, stooped. Often she found him looking at her with what might have been more than a healthy interest, but aside from that he kept his peace. Besides, Ivan had spent two years in secondary school (as much as Sophia) and she enjoyed conversing with him.

The third man, Georgi, was the troublemaker. Georgi was one of those plump young men with red cheeks, big, eager eyes, a voice somewhat too high. He was an avid talker, a boaster and a boor. In the beginning he showered attentions on Sophia. He insisted on drawing her wash basin at night, escorted her to breakfast every morning, told her in confidence of the conquests he had made over beautiful women (but not as beautiful as you, Sophia). He soon began to take liberties. He would sit—timorously at first, but with growing boldness—on the corner of her bed, talking with her at night after the others had retired, Ivan with his snores, Boris with his strong, deep breathing. And night after night, plump Georgi grew bolder.

He would reach out and touch Sophia, he would insist on tucking her in at night (let me be your big brother), he would awaken her in the morning with his hand heavy on her shoulder. Finally, one night at bedtime, she heard him conversing in low whispers with Ivan and Boris. She could not hear the words, but Boris looked at her with what she thought was surprise, I van nodded in an understanding way, and both of them left the room.

Sophia frowned. "What did you tell them, Georgi?"

"That we wanted to be alone one evening, of course."

"I never gave you any indication—"

"I could see it in your eyes, in the way you looked at me."

"Well, you had better call them back inside and go to bed."

Georgi shook his head, approached her.

"Georgi! Call them back or I will."

"No, you won't." Georgi followed her as she retreated into a corner of the room. When she reached the wall and could retreat no further, he placed his thick hands on her shoulders, drew her to him slowly. "You will call no one," he rasped.

SHE ducked under his arms, eluded him, was on the point of running to the door, throwing it open and shouting, when she reconsidered. If she did, she would be asking for quarter, gaining a temporary reprieve, inviting the same sort of thing all over again.

She crossed to the bed and sat down. "Come here, Georgi."

"Ah." he came to her.

She watched him warily, a soft flabby man not quite so tall as she was, but who nevertheless outweighed her by thirty or forty pounds. In his eagerness, he walked too fast, lost his footing and floated gently to the ceiling. Smiling as demurely as she could, Sophia reached up, circled his ankle with her hand.

"I never could get used to this weightlessness," Georgi admitted. "Be nice and pull me down."

"I will be nice. I will teach you a lesson."

He weighed exactly nothing. It was as simple as stretching. Sophia merely extended her arm upwards and Georgi's head hit the ceiling with a loud thunk. Georgi groaned. Sophia repeated the procedure, lowering her arm a foot—and Georgi with it—then raising it and bouncing his head off the ceiling.

"I don't understand," Georgi whined, trying to break free but only succeeding in thrashing his chubby arms foolishly.

"You haven't mastered weightlessness," Sophia smiled up at him. "I have. I said I would teach you a lesson. First make sure you have the strength of a man if you would play a man's game."

Still smiling, Sophia commenced spinning the hand that held Georgi's ankle. Arms and free leg flailing air helplessly, Georgi began to spin.

"Put me down!" he whined, a boy now, not even pretending to be a man. When Sophia shoved out gently and let his ankle go he did a neat flip in air and hung suspended, upside down, his feet near the ceiling, his head on a level with Sophia's shoulders. He cried.

She slapped his upside down face, carefully and without excitement, reddening the cheeks. "I was—only joking," he slobbered. "Call back our friends."

Sophia found one of the hard, airtight metal flasks they used for drinking in weightlessness. With one hand she opened the lid, with the other she grasped Georgi's shoulder and spun him in air, still upside down. She squirted the water in his face, and because he was upside down and yelling it made him choke and cough. When the container was empty she lowered Georgi gently to the floor.

Minutes later, she opened the door, summoned Boris and Ivan, who came into the room self-consciously. What they found was a thoroughly beaten Georgi sobbing on the floor. After that, Sophia had no trouble. Week after week of boredom followed and she almost wished Georgi or someone else would look for trouble...even if it were something she could not handle, for although she was stronger than average and more beautiful, she was still a woman first, and she knew if the right man...

"DID you know that radio communication is maintained between Earth and Mars?" the Alaric Arkalion on Mars asked Temple.

"Why, no. I never thought about it."

"It is, and I am in some difficulty."

"What's the matter?" Temple had grown to like Arkalion, despite the man's peculiarities." he had given up trying to figure him out, feeling that the only way he'd get anywhere was with Arkalion's cooperation.

"It's a long story which I'm afraid you would not altogether understand. The authorities on Earth don't think I belong here on the Nowhere Journey."

"Is that so? A mistake, huh? I sure am glad for you, Alaric."

"That's not the difficulty. It seems that there is the matter of impersonation, of violating some of the clauses in Public Law 1182. You're glad for me. I'm likely to go to prison."

"If it's that serious, how come they told you?"

"They didn't. But I—managed to find out. I won't go into details, Kit, but obviously, if I managed to embark for Nowhere when I didn't have to, then I wanted to go. Right?"

"I—uh, guess so. But why—?"

"That isn't the point. I still want to go. Not to Mars, but to Nowhere. I still can, despite what has happened, but I need help."

Temple said, "Anything I can do, I'll be glad to," and meant it. For one thing, he liked Arkalion. For another, Arkalion seemed to know more, much more than he would ever say—unless Temple could win his confidence. For a third, Temple was growing sick and tired of Mars with its drab ochre sameness (when he got to the surface, which was rarely), with its dank underground city, with its meaningless attention to meaningless detail. Either way, he figured there was no returning to Earth. If Nowhere meant adventure, as he suspected it might, it would be preferable. Mars might have been the other end of the galaxy for all its nearness to Earth, anyway.

"There is a great deal you can do. But you'll have to come with me."

"Where?" Temple demanded.

"Where you will go eventually. To Nowhere."

"Fine." And Temple smiled. "Why not now as well as later?"

"I'll be frank with you. If you go now, you go untrained. You may need your training. Undoubtedly, you will."

"You know a lot more than you want to talk about, don't you?"

"Frankly, yes...I am sorry, Kit."

"That's all right. You have your reasons. I guess if I go with you I'll find out soon enough, anyway."

Arkalion grinned. "You have guessed correctly. I am going to Nowhere, before they return me to Earth for prosecution under Public Law 1182. I cannot go alone, for it takes at least two to operate...well, you'll see."

"Count me in," said Temple.

"Remember, you may one day wish you had remained on Mars for your training."

"I'll take my chances. Mars is driving me crazy. All I do is think of Earth and Stephanie."

"Then come."

"Where are we going?"

"A long, long way off. It is unthinkably remote, this place called Nowhere."

Temple felt suddenly like a kid playing hooky from school. "Lead on," he said, almost jauntily. He knew he was leaving Stephanie still further behind, but had he been in prison on the next street to hers, he might as well have been a million miles away.

As for Arkalion—the thought suddenly struck Temple—Arkalion wasn't necessarily leaving his world further behind. Perhaps Arkalion was going home...

STEPHANIE picked up the phone eagerly. In the weeks

since her first meeting with Mrs. Draper of the C.E.L., the older woman had been a fountain of information and of hope for her. Stephanie for her part had taken over Mrs. Draper's job in her own section of Center City: she was busy contacting the two hundred mothers and fifty sweethearts of the Nowhere Journey which had taken Kit from her. And now Mrs. Draper had called with information.

"We've successfully combined forces with some of the less militant elements in both houses of Congress," Mrs. Draper told her over the phone. "Do you realize, my dear, this marks the first time the C.E.L. has managed to put something constructive through Congress? Until now we've been content merely to block legislation, such as an increase in the Nowhere contingent from…"

"Yes, Mrs. Draper. I know all that. But what about this constructive thing you've done."

"Well, my dear, don't count your chickens. But we have passed the bill, and we expect the President won't veto it. You see, the President has two nephews who…"

"I know. I know. What bill did you pass?"

"Unfortunately, it's somewhat vague. Ultimately, the Nowhere Commission must do the deciding, hut it does pave the way."

"For what, Mrs. Draper?"

"Hold onto your hat, my dear. The bill authorizes the Nowhere Commission to make as much of a study as it can of conditions—wherever our boys are sent."

"Oh." Stephanie was disappointed. "That won't get them back to us."

"No. You're right, it won't get them back to us. That isn't the idea at all, for there is more than one way to skin a cat, my dear. The Nowhere Commission will be studying conditions—"

"How can they? I thought everything was so hush-hush,

not even Congress knew anything about it."

"That was the first big hurdle we have apparently overcome. Anyway, they will be studying conditions with a view of determining if one girl—just one, mind you—can embark on the Nowhere journey as a pilot study and—"

"But I thought they could make the journey only once every seven-hundred-eighty days."

"Get Congress aroused and you can move mountains. It seems the expense entailed in a trip at any but those times is generally prohibitive, but when something special comes up—"

"It can be done! Mrs. Draper, how I love to talk with you!"

"See? There you go, my dear, counting your chickens. One girl will be sent, if the study indicates she can take it. One girl, Stephanie, and only after a study. She'd merely be a pilot case. But afterwards...ah, afterwards... Perhaps someday soon qualified women will be able to join their men in Nowhere."

"Mrs. Draper, I love you."

"Naturally, you will tell all this to prospective C.E.L. members. Now we have something concrete to work with."

"I know. And I will, I will, Mrs. Draper. By the way, how are they going to pick the girl, the one girl?"

"Don't count your chickens, for Heaven's sake! They haven't even studied the situation yet. Well, I'll call you, my dear."

Stephanie hung up, dressed, went about her canvassing. She thought happy thoughts all week.

"SHH! Quiet," cautioned Arkalion, leading the way down a flight of heavy-duty plastic stairs.

"How do you know your way around here so well?"

"I said quiet."

It was not so much, Temple realized, that Arkalion was really afraid of making noise. Rather, he did not want to answer questions.

Temple smiled in the semi-darkness, heard the steady drip-drip-drip of water off somewhere to his left. Eons before the coming of man on this stopover point to Nowhere, the Martian waters had retreated from the planet's ancient surface and seeped underground to carve, slow drop by drop, the caverns which honey-combed the planet. "You know your way around so well, I'd swear you were a Martian."

Arkalion's soft laugh carried far. "I said there was to be no noise. Please! As for the Martians, the only Martians are here all around you, the men of Earth. Ahh, here we are."

At the bottom of the flight of stairs Temple could see a door, metallic, giving the impression of strength without great weight. Arkalion paused a moment, did something with a series of levers, shook his head impatiently, started all over again.

"What's that for?" Temple wanted to know.

"What do you think? It is a combination lock, with five million possible combinations. Do you want to be here for all of eternity?"

"No."

"Then quiet."

Vaguely, Temple wondered why the door wasn't guarded.

"With a lock like this," Arkalion explained, as if he had read Temple's thought, "they need no other precaution. It is assumed that only authorized personnel know the combination."

Then had Arkalion come this way before? It seemed the only possible assumption. But when? And how? "Here we are," said Arkalion.

The door swung in toward them.

Temple strode forward, found himself in a great bare hall,

surprisingly well lighted. After the dimness of the caverns, he hardly could see.

"Don't stand there scowling and fussing with your eyes. There is one additional precaution—an alarm at Central Headquarters. We have about five minutes, no more."

AT one end of the bare hall stood what to Temple looked for all the world like an old-fashioned telephone booth, except that its walls were completely opaque. On the wall adjacent to it was a single lever with two positions marked "hold" and "transport". The lever stood firmly in the "hold" position.

"You sure you want to come?" Arkalion demanded.

"Yes, I told you that."

"Good. I have no time to explain. I will enter the conveyor."

"Conveyor?"

"This booth. You will wait until the door is shut, then pull the lever down. That is all there is to it, but, as you can see, it is a two-man operation."

"But how do I—"

"Haste, haste! There are similar controls at the other end. You pull the lever, wait two minutes, and enter the conveyor yourself. I will fetch you—if you are sure."

"I'm sure, dammit!"

"Remember, you go without training, without the opportunity everyone else has."

"You already told me that. Mars is halfway to eternity. Mars is limbo. If I can't go back to Earth I want to go—well, to Nowhere. There are too many ghosts here, too many memories with nothing to do."

Arkalion shrugged, entered the booth. "Pull the lever," he said, and shut the door.

Temple reached up, grasped the lever firmly in his hand,

yanked it. It slid smoothly to the position marked "transport." Temple heard nothing, saw nothing, began to think the device, whatever it was, did not work. Did Arkalion somehow get moved inside the booth?

Temple thought he heard footfalls on the stairs outside. Soon, faintly, he could hear voices. Someone banged on the door to the hall. Licking dry lips, Temple opened the booth, peered inside.

Empty.

The voices clamored, fists pounded on the door. Something clicked. Tumblers fell. The door to the great, bright hall sprung outward. Someone rushed in at Temple, who met him savagely with a short, chopping blow to his jaw. The man, temporarily blinded by the dazzling light, stumbled back in the path of his fellows.

Temple darted into the booth, the conveyor, and slammed it shut. Fingers clawed on the outside.

A sound almost too intense to be heard rang in Temple's ears. He lost consciousness instantly.

CHAPTER SIX

"WHAT a cockeyed world," said Alaric Arkalion Sr. to his son. "You certainly can't plan on anything, even if you do have more money than you'll ever possibly need in a lifetime."

"Don't feel like that," said young Alaric. "I'm not in prison any longer, am I?"

"No. But you're not free of the Nowhere Journey, either. There is an unheralded special trip to Nowhere, two weeks from today, I have been informed."

"Oh?"

"Yes, oh. I have also been informed that you will be on it. You didn't escape after all, Alaric."

"Oh. Oh!"

"What bothers me most is that scoundrel Smith somehow managed to escape. They haven't found him yet, I have also been informed. And since my contract with him calls for ten million dollars for services rendered, I'll have to pay."

"But he didn't prevent me from—"

"I can't air this thing, Alaric! But listen, son: when you go where you are going, you're liable to find another Alaric Arkalion, your double. Of course, that would be Smith. If you can get him to cut his price in half because of what has happened, I would be delighted. If you could somehow manage to wring his neck, I would be even more delighted. Ten million dollars—for nothing."

"I'M so excited," murmured Mrs. Draper. Stephanie watched her on one of the new televiewers, recently installed in place of the telephone.

"What is it?"

"Our bill has been passed by a landslide majority in both houses of Congress!"

"Ooo!" cried Stephanie.

"Not very coherent, my dear, but those are my sentiments exactly. In two weeks there will be a Journey to Nowhere, a special one which will include, among its passengers, a woman."

"But the study that had to be made—?"

"It's already been made. From what I gather, they can't take it very far. Most of their conclusions had to be based on supposition. The important thing, though, is this: a woman will be sent. The way the O.E.L. figures it, my dear, is that a woman falling in the twenty-one to twenty-six age group should be chosen, a woman who meets all the requirements placed upon the young men."

"Yes," said Stephanie. "Of course. And I was just thinking that I would be—"

"Remember those chickens!" cautioned Mrs. Draper. "We already have one hundred seventy-seven volunteers who'd claw each other to pieces for a chance to go."

"Wrong," Stephanie said, smiling. "You now have one hundred seventy-eight."

"Room for only one, my dear. Only one, you know."

"Then cross the others off your list. I'm already packing my bag."

WHEN Temple regained consciousness, it was with the feeling that no more than a split second of time had elapsed. So much had happened so rapidly that, until now, he hadn't had time to consider it.

Arkalion had vanished.

Vanished—he could use no other word. He was there, standing in the booth—and then he wasn't. Simple as that.

Now you see it, now you don't. And goodbye, Arkalion.

But goodbye Temple, too. For hadn't Temple entered the same booth, waiting but a second until Arkalion activated the mechanism at the other end? And certainly Temple wasn't in the booth now. He smiled at the ridiculously simple logic of his thoughts. He stood in an open field, the blades of grass rising to his knees, as much brilliant purple as they were green. Waves of the grass, stirred like tide by the gentle wind, and hills rolling off toward the horizon in whichever direction he turned. Far away, the undulating hills lifted to a half soft mauve sky. A somber red sun with twice Sol's apparent disc but half its brightness hung midway between zenith and horizon completing the picture of peaceful other-worldliness.

Wherever this was, it wasn't Earth—or Mars.

Nowhere?

Temple shrugged, started walking. He chose his direction at random, crushing an easily discernible path behind him in the surprisingly brittle grass. The warm sun baked his back comfortably, the soft-stirring wind caressed his cheeks. Of Arkalion he found not a trace.

Two hours later Temple reached the hills and started climbing their gentle slopes. It was then that he saw the figure approaching on the run. It took him fully half a minute to realize that the runner was not human.

AFTER months of weightless inactivity, things started to happen for Sophia. The feeling of weight returned, but weight as she never had felt it before. It was as if someone was sitting on every inch of her body, crushing her down. It made her gasp, forced her eyes shut and, although she could not see it, contorted her face horribly. She lost consciousness, coming to some time later with a dreadful feeling of loginess. Someone swam into her vision dimly, stung her arm briefly with a needle. She slept.

She was on a table, stretched out, with lights glaring down at her. She heard voices.

"The new system is far better than testing, comrade."

"Far more efficient, far more objective. Yes."

"The brain emits electromagnetic vibration. Strange, is it not, that no one before ever imagined it could tell a story. A completely accurate story two years of testing could not give us."

"In Russia we have gone far with the biological, psychological sciences. The West flies high with physics. Give them Mars; bah, they can have Mars."

"True, Comrade. The journey to Jupiter is greater, the time consumed is longer, the cost, more expensive. But here on Jupiter we can do something they cannot do on Mars."

"I know."

"We can make supermen. Supermen, comrade. A wedding of Nietzsche and Marx."

"Careful. Those are dangerous thoughts."

"Merely an allusion, comrade. Merely a harmless allusion. But you take an ordinary human being and train him on Jupiter, speeding his time-sense and metabolic rate tremendously with certain endocrine secretions so that one day is as a month to him. You take him and subject him to big Jupiter's pull of gravity, more than twice Earth's—and in three weeks you have, yes—you have a superman."

"The Woman wakes."

"Shhh. Do not frighten her."

Sophia stretched, every muscle in her body aching. Slowly, as in a dream, she sat up. It required strength, the mere act of pulling her torso upright!

"What have you done to me?" she cried, focussing her still-dim vision on the two men.

"Nothing, comrade. Relax."

Sophia turned slowly on the table, got one long shapely leg

draped over its edge.

"Careful, comrade."

What were they warning her about? She merely wanted to get up and stretch; perhaps then she would feel better. Her toe touched the floor, she swung her other leg over, aware of but ignoring her nakedness.

"A good specimen."

"Oh, yes, comrade. So this time they send a woman among the others. Well, we shall do our work. Look—see the way she is formed, so lithe, loose-limbed, agile. See the toning of the muscles? Her beauty will remain, comrade, but Jupiter shall make an amazon of her."

SOPHIA had both feet on the floor now. She was breathing hard, felt suddenly sick to her stomach. Placing both her hands on the table edge, she pushed off and staggered for two or three paces. She crumpled, buckling first at the knees then the waist, and fell in a writhing heap.

"Pick her up."

Hands under her arms, tugging. She came off the floor easily, dimly aware that someone carried her hundred and thirty pounds effortlessly. "Put me down!" she cried. "I want to try again. I am crippled, crippled! You have crippled me…"

"Nothing of the sort, comrade. You are tired, weak, and Jupiter's gravity field is still too strong for you. Little by little, though, your muscles will strengthen to Jupiter's demands. Gravity will keep them from bulging, expanding; but every muscle fiber in you will have twice, three times its original strength. Are you excited?"

"I am tired and sick. I want to sleep. What is Jupiter?"

"Jupiter is a planet circling the sun at—never mind, comrade. You have much to learn, but you can assimilate it with much less trouble in your sleep. Go ahead, sleep."

Sophia retched, was sick. It had been years since she cried. But naked, afraid, bewildered, she cried herself to sleep.

Things happened while she slept, many things. Certain endocrine extracts accelerated her metabolism astonishingly. Within half an hour her heart was pumping blood through her body two hundred beats per minute. An hour later it reached its full rate, almost one thousand contractions every sixty seconds. All her other metabolic functions increased accordingly, and Sophia slept deeply for a week of subjective time—in hours. The same machine which had gleaned everything from her mind far more accurately than a battery of tests, a refinement of the electro-encephalogram, was now played in reverse, giving back to Sophia everything it had taken plus electrospool after electrospool of science, mathematics, logic, economics, history (Marxion, these last two), languages (including English), semantics and certain specialized knowledge she would need later on the Stalintrek.

Still sleeping, Sophia was bathed in a warm whirlpool of soothing liquid; rubbed, massaged, her muscle toning begun while she rested and regained her strength. Three hours later, objective time, she awoke with a headache and with more thoughts spinning around madly inside her brain than she ever knew existed. Gingerly, she tried standing again, lifting herself nude and dripping wet from a tub of steaming amber stuff. She stood, stretched, permitted her fright to vanish with a quick wave of vertigo, which engulfed her. She had been fed intravenously, but a tremendous hunger possessed her. Before eating, however, she was to find herself in a gymnasium, the air close and stifling. She was massaged again, told to do certain exercises that seemed simple but which she found extremely difficult, forced to run until she thought she would collapse, with her legs, dragging like lead.

She understood, now. Somehow she knew she was on

Jupiter, the fifth and largest planet, where the force of gravity is so much greater than on Earth that it is an effort even to walk. She also knew that her metabolic rate had been accelerated beyond all comprehension and that in a comparatively short time—objective time—she would have thrice her original strength. All this she knew without knowing how she knew, and that was the most staggering fact of all. She did what her curt instructors bid, then dragged her aching muscles and her headache into a dining room where tired, forlorn-looking men sat around eating. Well, the food at least was good. Sophia attacked it ravenously.

IT did not take Temple long to realize that the creature running downhill at him, leaving a crushed and broken wake in the purple and green grass, was not human. At first Temple toyed with the idea of a man on horseback, for the creature ran on four limbs and had two left over as arms. Temple gaped.

The whole thing was one piece!

Centaur?

Hardly. Too small, for one thing. No bigger than a man, despite the three pairs of limbs. And then Temple had time to gape no longer, for the creature, whatever it was, flashed past him at what he now had to consider a gallop.

More followed. Different. Temple stared and stared. One could have been a great, sentient hoop, rolling downhill and gathering momentum. If he carried the wheel analogy further, a huge eye stared at him from where the hub would have been. Something else followed with kangaroo leaps. One thick-thewed leg propelled it in tremendous, fifteen-foot hopping strides while its small, flapper-like arms beat the air prodigiously.

Legions of creatures. All fantastically different. *I'm going crazy,* Temple thought, then said it aloud. "I'm going crazy."

Theorizing thus, he heard a whir overhead, whirled, looked up. Something was poised a dozen feet off the ground, a large, box-like object seven or eight feet across, rotors spinning above it. That, at least, he could understand. A helicopter.

"I'm lowering a ladder, Kit. Swing aboard."

Arkalion's voice.

Stunned enough to accept anything he saw, Temple waited for the rope ladder to drop, grasped its end, and climbed. He swung his legs over a sill, found himself in a neat little cabin with Arkalion, who hauled the ladder in and did something to the controls. They sped away. Temple had one quick moment of lucid thought before everything that had happened in the last few moments shoved logic aside. What he had observed looked for all the world like a footrace.

"Where the hell *are* we?" Temple demanded breathlessly.

Arkalion smiled. "Where do you think? Journey's end. Welcome to Nowhere, Kit. Welcome to the place where all your questions can be answered because there's no going back. Sorry I set you down in that field by mistake, incidentally. Those things sometimes happen."

"Can I just throw the questions at you?"

"If you wish. It isn't really necessary, for you will be indoctrinated when we get you over to Earth city where you belong."

"What do you mean, there's no going back? I thought they had a rotation system, which for one reason or another, wasn't practical at the moment. That doesn't sound like no going back, ever."

Arkalion grunted, shrugged. "Have it your way. I *know.*"

"Sorry. Shoot."

"Just how far do you think you have come?"

"Search me. Some other star system, maybe?"

"Maybe. Clean across the galaxy, Kit."

Temple whistled softly. "It isn't something you can grasp just by hearing it. Across the galaxy…"

"That isn't too important just now. How long did you think the journey took?"

Temple nodded eagerly. "That's what gets me. It was amazing, Alaric. Really amazing. The whole trip couldn't have taken more than a moment or two. I don't get it. Did we slip out of normal pace into some other—uh, continuum, and speed across the length of the galaxy like that?"

"The answer to your question is yes. But your statement is way off. The journey did not take seconds, Kit."

"No? Instantaneous?"

"Far more than seconds. To reach here from Earth you traveled five thousand years."

"What?"

"More correctly, it was five thousand years ago that you left Mars. You would need a time machine to return, and there is no such thing. The Earth you know is the length of the galaxy and five thousand years behind you."

CHAPTER SEVEN

IT could have been a city in New England, or maybe Wisconsin. Main Street stretched for half a mile from Town Hall to the small department store. Neon tubing brightened every storefront, busy proprietors could be seen at work through the large plate glass windows. There was the bustle you might expect on any Main Street in New England or Wisconsin, but you could not draw the parallel indefinitely.

There were only men. No women.

The hills in which the town nestled were too purple—not purple with distance, but the natural color of the grass.

A somber red sun hung in the pale mauve sky.

This was Earth City, Nowhere.

Arkalion had deposited Temple in the nearby hills, promised they would see one another again. "It may not be so soon," Arkalion had said, "but what's the difference? You'll spend the rest of your life here. You realize you are lucky, Kit. If you hadn't come, you would have been dead these five thousand years. Well, good luck."

Dead—five thousand years. The Earth as he knew it, dust. Stephanie, a fifty generation corpse. Nowhere was right. End of the universe.

Temple shuffled his feet, trudged on into town. A man passed him on the street, stooped, gray-haired. The man nodded, did a mild double take. *I'm an unfamiliar face*, Temple thought.

"Howdy," he said. "I'm new here."

"That's what I thought, stranger. Know just about everyone in these here parts, I do, and I said to myself, now there's a newcomer. Funny you didn't come in the regular way."

"I'm here," said Temple.

"Yeah. Funny thing, you get to know everyone. Eh, what you say your name was?"

"Christopher Temple."

"Make it my business to know everyone. The neighborly way, I always say. Temple, eh? We have one here."

"One what?"

"Another fellow name of Temple. Jase Temple, son."

"I'll be damned!" Temple cried, smiling suddenly. "I will be damned. Tell me, old timer, where can I find him?"

"Might be anyplace. Town's bigger'n it looks. I tell you, though, Jase Temple's our coordinator. You'll find him there, the coordinator's office. Town Hall, down the end of the street."

"I already passed it," Temple told the old man. "And thanks."

Temple's legs carried him at a brisk pace, past the row of storefronts and down to the Town Hall. He read a directory, climbed a flight of stairs, found a door marked:

JASON TEMPLE

Earth City Coordinator

Heart pounding, Temple knocked, heard someone call, "Come in."

He pushed the door in and stared at his brother, just rising to face him.

"KIT! Kit! What are you doing—you took the journey too!"

Jason ran to him, clasped his shoulders, pounded them. "I don't believe it…I don't believe it! They drafted you for the Nowhere Journey, too. And you're here, you're actually *here!*" A big smile came over his face. "And you sure are looking fit. Kit, you could have knocked me over with half a feather, coming in like this."

"You're looking great too, Jase," Kit lied. He hadn't seen his brother in five years and had never expected to see him again. But the Jason Temple he remembered was a full-faced, smiling man somewhat taller than himself, somewhat broader across the shoulders. However, the man who stood before him easily looked forty-five years old, maybe fifty, but hardly a youthful kid out of his twenties. He had fierce, smoldering eyes, gaunt cheeks, and graying hair. Kit's instant impression was that his older brother seemed to be a bundle of restless, nervous energy.

"Sit down, Kit, sit down. Start talking, kid brother. Start talking and don't stop till next week. Tell me everything. Everything! Tell me about the blue sky and the moon at night and the way the ocean looks on a windy day and…"

"Five years," said Kit. "Five years."

"Five thousand, you mean," Jason reminded him. "It hardly seems possible. How are the folks, Kit?"

"Mom's fine. Pop too. He's sporting a new Chambers Converto. You should see him, Jase. Sharp."

"And Ann?" Jason looked at him hopefully. Ann had been Jason's Stephanie—but for the Nowhere Journey they would have married.

"Ann's married," Temple said softly.

"Oh…Oh. That's swell, Kit. Really swell. I mean, what the hell, a girl shouldn't wait forever. I told her not to, anyway."

"She waited four years, then met a guy and—"

"A nice guy?"

"The best," said Temple. "You'd like him."

Temple saw the vague hurt come to Jason's smoldering eyes. Then it was the same. One part of Jason wanted her to remain his over an unthinkable gap, another part wanted her to live a good, full life.

"I'm glad," said Jason. "Can't expect a girl to wait without hope…"

"Then there's no hope we'll ever get back?"

Jason laughed harshly. "You tell me. Earth isn't merely sixty thousand light years away. Kit, do you know what a light year is"

Temple said he thought he did.

"Sixty thousand of them. A dozen eternities. But the Earth we know is also dead. Dead five thousand years. The folks, Center City, Ann, her husband—all dust. Five thousand years old…" His voiced trailed off for a moment, then he shook his head slowly, a half smile coming over his face. "Don't mind me, little brother."

"Sure. Sure, I understand." But Temple didn't—not really. You couldn't take five thousand years and chuck them out the window in what seemed the space of a heart beat and then realize they were gone permanently, forever. Not a period of time as long as all of recorded civilization—you couldn't take it, tack it on after 1992 and accept it. Somehow, Temple realized, the five thousand years were harder to swallow than the sixty thousand light years.

"Well," with a visible effort, Jason snapped out of his reverie. Temple accepted a cigarette gratefully, his first in a long time. *My first in fifty centuries!* he thought bitterly, burrowing deeper into a funk.

"Well," said Jason, "I'm acting like a prize boob. How selfish can I get? There must be an awful lot you'd like to know, Kit."

"That's all right. I was told I'd be indoctrinated."

"Ordinarily, you would. But there's no shipment now, none for another three months. Say, how the devil did you get here?"

"That's a long story. Nowhere Journey, same as you, with a little assist to speed things up on Mars. Jase, tell me this:

what are we doing here? What is everyone doing here? What's the Nowhere Journey all about? What kind of a glorified footrace did I see a while ago, with a bunch of creatures out of the telio science fiction shows?"

JASON put his own cigarette out, changed his mind, lit another one. "Sort of like the old joke, where does an alien go to register?"

"Sort of."

"It's a big universe," said Jason, evidently starting at the beginning of something.

"I'm just beginning to learn how big!"

"It would be pretty unimaginative of mankind to consider itself the only sentient form of life, Earth the only home of intelligence, both from a scientific and a religious point of view. We kind of expected to find—neighbors out in space. Kit, the sky is full of stars, most stars have planets. The universe crawls with life, all sorts of life, all sorts of intelligent life. In short, we are not alone. It would be sort of like taking the jet-shuttle from Washington to New York during the evening rush and expecting to be the only one aboard. In reality, you're lucky to get breathing space.

"There are biped intelligences, like humans. There are radial intelligences, one-legged species, tall, gangling creatures, squat ones, pancake ones, giants, dwarfs. There are green skins and pink skins and coal black—and yes, no skins. There are...but you get the idea."

"Uh-huh."

"Strangely enough, most of these intelligences are on about the same developmental level. It's as if the Creator turned everything on at once, like a race, and said, 'okay, guys...get started.' Maybe it's because, as scientists figure, the whole universe got wound up and started working as a unit. I don't know. Anyway, that's the way it is. All the intelligences worth talking about are on about the same cultural level. Atomics, crude spaceflight, wars they can't handle.

"And this is interesting, Kit. Most of 'em are bipedal. Not really human, not fully human. You can see the difference. But seventy-five percent of the races I've encountered have had basic similarities. A case of the Creator trying to figure out the best of all possible life-patterns and coming up with this one. Offers a wide range for action, for adaptation, stuff like that. Anyway, I'm losing track of things."

"Take it easy. From what you tell me I have all the time in the world."

"Well, I said all the races are developmentally parallel. That's almost true. One of them is not. One of them is so far ahead that the rest of us have hardly reached the crawling stage by comparison. One of them is the Super Race, Kit.

"Their culture is old, incredibly old. So old, in fact, that some of us figure it's been hanging around since before the Universe took shape. Maybe that's why all the others are on one level, a few thousand million years behind the Super Race.

"So, take this Super Race. For some reason we can't understand, it seems to be on the skids. That's just figurative. Maybe it's dying out, maybe it wants to pack up and leave the galaxy altogether, maybe it's got other undreamed of business other undreamed of places. Anyway, it wants out. But it's got an eon-old storehouse of culture and maybe it figures someone ought to have access to that and keep the galaxy in running order. But who? That's the problem. Who gets all this information, a million million generations of scientific problems, all carefully worked out? Who, among all the parallel races on all the worlds of the Universe? That's quite a problem, even for our Super Race boys.

"You'd think they'd have ways to solve it, though. With

calculating machines or whatever will follow calculating machines after Earthmen and all the others find the next faltering step after a few thousand years. Or with plain horse sense and logic, developed to a point—after millions of years at it—where it never fails. Or solve the problem with something we've never heard of, but solve it anyway."

"What's all this got to do with—? I mean, it's an interesting story and when I get a chance to digest it I'll probably start gasping, but what about Nowhere and..."

"I'm coming to that. Kit, what would you say if I told you that the most intelligent race the Universe has ever produced solves the biggest problem ever handed anyone—by playing games?"

"I'D say you better continue."

"That's the purpose of Nowhere, Kit. Every planet, every race has its Nowhere. We all come here and we play games. Planet with the highest score at the end of God knows how long wins the Universe, with all the science and the wisdom needed to fashion that universe into a dozen different kinds of heaven. And to decide all this, we play games.

"Don't get the wrong idea. I'm not complaining. If the Superboys say we play, then we play. I'd take their word for it if they told me I had fifteen heads. But it's the sort of thing that doesn't let you get much sleep. Oh, Earth has a right to be proud of its record. United North America is in second place on a competition that's as wide as the Universe. But we're not first. Second. And I have a hunch from what's been going on around here that the games are drawing to a close.

"Fantastic, isn't it? Out of thousands of entrants, we're good enough to place second. But some planet out near the star Deneb has us hopelessly outclassed. We might as well get the booby prize. They'll win and own the Universe—us included."

Jason had leaned forward as he spoke, and was sitting on the edge of his chair now. The room was comfortably cool, but sweat beaded his forehead and dripped from his chin.

Kit lit another cigarette, inhaling deeply. "You said the United States—North America—was second. I thought this was a planet-wide competition, planet against planet."

"Earth is the one exception I've been able to find. The Deneb planet heads the list, then comes North America. After that, the planet of a star I never heard of. In fourth place is the Soviet Union."

"I'll be damned," said Temple. "Well, okay. Mind if I store that away for future reference? I've got another question. What kind of—uh, games do we play?"

"You name it. Mental contests. Scientific problems to be worked out with laboratories built to our specifications. Emotional problems with scores of men driven neurotic or worse every year. Problems of adaptability. Responses to environmental challenge. Stamina contests. Tests of strength, of endurance. Tests to determine depths of emotion. Tests to determine objectivity in what should be an objective situation. But the way everything is organized it's almost like a giant-sized, never ending Olympic Games, complete with some cockeyed sports events too, by the way."

"With all the pageantry, too?"

"No. But that's another story."

"Anyway, what I saw *was* a footrace! And sorry, Jase, but I have another question."

Jason shrugged, spread his hands wide.

"How come all this talk about rotation? It isn't possible, not with a fifty century gap."

"I know. They just let us in on that little deal a couple of years ago. Till then, we didn't know. We thought it was distance only. In time, after all this was over, we could go home. That's what we thought," Jason said bitterly. "Actually, it's twice five thousand years. Five to come here, five to return. Ten thousand years separate us from the Earth we know, and even if we could go home, that wouldn't be going home at all—to Earth ten thousand years in the future.

"Oh, they had us hoodwinked. Afraid we might say no or something. They never mentioned the length or duration of the trip. I don't understand it, none of us do and we have some top scientists here. Something to do with suspended animation, with contra-terrene matter, with teleportation, something about latent extra-sensory powers in everyone, about the ability to break down an object—or a creature or a man—to its component atoms, to reverse—that's the word, reverse—those atoms and send them spinning off into space as contra-terrene matter.

"It all boils down to putting a man in a machine on Mars, pulling a lever, materializing him here five thousand years later." Jason smiled with only a trace of humor. "Any questions?"

"About a thousand," said Temple. "I—"

SOMETHING buzzed on Jason's desk and Temple watched him pick up a microphone, say: "Coordinator speaking. What's up?"

The voice that answered, clear enough to be in the room with them and without the faintest trace of mechanical or electrical transfer, spoke in a strange, liquid-syllabled language Temple had never heard. Jason responded in the same language, with an apparent ease that surprised Temple—until he remembered that his brother had always had a knack of picking up foreign languages. Maybe that was why he held the Coordinator's job—whatever it was he coordinated.

There was fluency in the way Jason spoke, and alarm. The trouble-lines etched deeply on his face, stood out sharply, and his eyes—if possible—grew more intense. "Well," he said, putting the mike down and staring at Temple without seeing him, "I'm afraid that does it."

"What's the trouble?"

"Everything."

"Anything I can do?"

"Item. The Superboys have discovered that Earth has two contingents here—the Soviets and us. They're mad. Item. Something will be done about it. Item. Soviet Russia has made a suggestion, or that is, its people here. They will put forth a champion to match one of our own choosing in the toughest grind of all, something to do with responding to environmental challenge, which doesn't mean a hell of a lot unless you happen to know something about it. Shall I go on?"

And, when Temple nodded avidly. "We automatically lose by default. One of the rules of that particular game is that the contestant must be a newcomer. It's the sort of game you have to know nothing about, and incidentally, it's also the sort of game a man can get killed at. Well, the Soviets have a whole contingent of newcomers to pick from. We don't have any. As the Superboys see it, that's our own tough luck. We lose by default."

"It seems to me—"

"How can anything seem to you?' You're new here...I'm sorry Kit. What were you saying?"

"No. Go ahead."

"That's only the half of it. Right after Russia takes our place and we're scratched off the list, the games go into their final phase. That was the rumor all along, and it's just been confirmed. Interesting to see what they do with all the contestants after the games are over, after there's no more Nowhere Journey."

"We could go back where we came from."

"Ten thousand years in the future?"

"I'm not afraid."

"Well, anyway, the Soviets put up a man, we can't match him. So it looks like the U.S.S.R. represents Earth officially. Not that it matters. We hardly have the chance of a very slushy snowball in a very hot hell. But still—"

"Our contestant, this guy who meets the Russian's challenge, has to be a newcomer?"

"That's what I said. Well, we can close up shop, I guess."

"You made a mistake. You said no newcomers have arrived. I'm here, Jase. I'm your man. Bring on your Russian Bear." Temple smiled grimly.

CHAPTER EIGHT

"YOU got to hand it to Temple's kid brother."

"Yeah. Cool as ice cubes."

"Are you guys kidding? He doesn't know what's in store for him, that's all."

"Do *you?*"

"Now that you mention it, no. Isn't a man here who can say for sure what kind of environmental challenges he'll have to respond to. Hypno-surgery sees to it the guys who went through the thing won't talk about it. As if that isn't security enough, the subject's got to be a brand new arrival!"

"Shhh! Here he comes."

The brothers Temple entered Earth City's one tavern quietly, but on their arrival all the speculative talk subsided. The long bar, built to accommodate half a hundred pairs of elbows comfortably, gleamed with a luster unfamiliar to Temple. It might have been marble, but marble translucent rather than opaque, giving a beautiful three-dimensional effect to the surface patterns.

"What will it be?" Jason demanded.

"Whatever you're drinking is fine."

Jason ordered two scotches, neat, and the brothers drank. When Jason got a refill he started talking. "Does T.A.T. mean anything to you, Kit?"

"Tat? Umm—no. Wait a minute! T.A.T. Isn't that some kind of projective psychological test?"

"That's it. You're shown a couple of dozen pictures, more or less ambiguous, never cut and dry. Each one comes from a different stratum of the social environment, and you're told to create a dramatic situation, a story, for each picture. From your stories, for which you draw on your whole background as a human being, the psychometrician should be able to build a picture of your personality and maybe find out what, if anything, is bothering you."

"What's that to do with this response to environmental challenge thing?"

"Well," said Jason, drinking a third scotch, "the Super Boys have evolved T.A.T. to its ultimate. T.A.T.—that stands for Thematic Apperception Test. But in E.C.R.— environmental challenge and response, you don't see a picture and create a dramatic story around it. Instead, you get thrust into the picture, the situation, and you have to work out the solution—or suffer whatever consequences the particular environmental challenge has in store for you."

"I think I get you. But it's all make believe, huh?"

"That's the hell of it," Jason told him. "No, it's not. It is and it isn't. I don't know."

"You make it perfectly clear," Temple smiled. "The red-headed boy combed his brown hair, wishing it weren't blond."

Jason shrugged. "I'm sorry. For reasons you already know, the E.C.R. isn't very clear to me—or to anyone. You're not actually in the situation in a physical sense, but it can affect you physically. You feel you're there, you actually live everything that happens to you, getting injured if an injury occurs...and dying if you get killed. It's permanent, although you might actually be sleeping at the time. So, whether it's real or not is a question for philosophy. From your point of view, from the point of view of someone going through it, it's real."

"So I become part of this—uh, game in about an hour."

"Right. You and whoever the Russians offer as your competition. No one will blame you if you want to back out, Kit; from what you tell me, you haven't even been adequately trained on Mars."

"If you draw on the entire background of your life for this E.C.R., then you don't need training. Shut up and stop worrying. I'm not backing out of anything."

"I didn't think you would, not if you're still as much like your old man as you used to be. Kit...good luck."

THE fact that the technicians working around him were Earthmen permitted Temple to relax a little. Probably, it was planned that way, for entering the huge white cube of a building and ascending to the twelfth level on a moving ramp Temple had spotted many figures, not all of them human. If he had been strapped to the table by unfamiliar aliens, if the scent of alien flesh—or nonflesh—had been strong in the room, if the fingers—or appendages—that greased his temples and clamped an electrode to each one had not felt like human fingers, if the men talking to him had spoken in voices too harsh or too sibilant for human vocal chords—if all that had been the case, whatever composure still remained his would have vanished.

"I'm Dr. Olson," said one white-gowned figure. "If any injuries occur while you lie here, I'm permitted to render first aid."

"The same for limited psychotherapy," said a shorter, heavier man. "Though a fat lot of good it does when we never know what's bothering you, and don't have the time to work on it even if we did know."

"In short," said a third man who failed to identify himself, "you may consider yourself as the driver of one of those midget rocket racers. Do they still have them on Earth? Good. You are the driver, and we here in this room are the mechanics waiting in your pit. If anything goes wrong, you can pull out of the race temporarily and have it repaired. But in this particular race there is no pulling out, all repairs are strictly of a first aid nature and must be done while you continue whatever you are doing. If you break your finger and find a splint appearing on it miraculously, don't say you weren't warned."

"Best of luck to you, young man," said the psychotherapist.

"Here we go," said the doctor, finding the large vein on the inside of Temple's forearm and plunging a needle into it.

Temple's senses whirled instantly, but as his vision clouded he thought he saw a large, complex device swing down from the ceiling and bathe his head in warming radiation. He blinked, squinted, but could see nothing but a swirling, cloudy opacity.

APPROXIMATELY two seconds later, Sophia Androvna Petrovitch watched as the white-gowned comrade tied a rubber strap around her arm, waited for the vein to swell with blood, then forced a needle in through its thick outer layer. Was that a nozzle overhead? No, rather a lens, for from it came amber warmth...that soon faded—with everything else—into thick, churning fog...

Temple was abruptly aware of running, plunging headlong and blindly through the fiercest storm he had ever seen. Gusts of wind whipped at him furiously. Rain cascaded down in drenching torrents. Foliage, brambles, branches struck against his face; mud sucked at his feet. Big animal shapes lumbered by in the green gloom, as frightened by the storm as was Temple.

His head darted this way and that, his eyes could see the gnarled tree trunks, the dense greenery, the lianas, creepers and vines of a tropical rain forest—but dimly. Green murk swirled in like thick smoke with every gust of wind, with the rain obscuring vision almost completely.

Temple ran until his lungs burned and he thought he must

exhale fire. His leaden feet fought the mud with growing difficulty for every stride he took. He ran wildly and in no set direction, convinced only that he must find shelter or perish. Twice he crashed bodily into trees, twice stumbled to his knees only to pull himself upright again, sucking air painfully into his lungs and cutting out in a fresh direction.

He ran until his legs balked. He fell, collapsing first at the knees, then the waist, then flopping face down in the mud. Something prodded his back as he fell and reaching behind him weakly Temple was aware for the first time that a bow and a quiver of arrows hung suspended from his shoulders by a strong leather thong. He wore nothing but a loin cloth of some nameless animal skin and he wondered idly if he had slain the animal with the weapon he carried. Yet when he tried to recollect he found he could not. He remembered nothing but his frantic flight through the rain forest, as if all his life he had run in a futile attempt to leave the rain behind him.

Now as he lay there, the mud sucking at his legs, his chest, his armpits, he could not even remember his name. Did he have one? Did he have a life before the rain forest? Then why did he forget?

A sense not fully developed in man and called intuition by those who fail to understand it made him prop his head up on his hands and squint through the downpour. There was something off there in the foliage...someone...

A woman.

Temple's breath caught in his throat sharply. The woman stood half a dozen paces off, observing him coolly with hands on flanks. She stood tall and straight despite the storm, and from the trim ankles to the long, lithe legs to the flaring loin-clothed hips, to the supple waist and tawny skin of fine bare breasts and shoulders, to the proud, haughty face and long dark hair loose in the storm and glistening with rain, she was magnificent. Her long, bronzed body gleamed with wetness and Temple realized she was as tall as he, a wild beautiful goddess of the jungle. She was part of the storm and he accepted her—but strangely, with the same fear the storm evoked. She would make a lover the whole world might relish (what world, Temple thought in confusion?) but she would also make a terrible foe.

And foe she was...

"I want your bow and arrows," she told him.

TEMPLE wanted to suggest they share the weapon, but somehow he knew in this world which was like a dream and could tell him things the way a dream would and yet was vividly real, that the woman would share nothing with anybody.

"They are mine," Temple said, climbing to his knees. He remembered the animal-shapes lumbering by in the storm and he knew that he and the animals would both stalk prey when the storm subsided and he would need the bow and arrows.

The woman moved toward him with a liquid motion beautiful to behold, and for the space of a heartbeat Temple watched her come. "I will take them," she said.

Temple wasn't sure if she could or not, and although she was a woman he feared her strangely. Again, it was as if something in this dream-world real world could tell him more than he should know.

Making up his mind, Temple sprang to his feet, whirled about and ran. He was plunging through the wild storm once more, blinded by the occasional flashes of jagged green lightning, deafened by the peals of thunder that followed. And he was being pursued.

Minutes, hours, more than hours—for an eternity Temple ran. A reservoir of strength he never knew he possessed provided the energy for each painful step and running through the storm seemed the most natural thing in the world to him. But there came a time when his strength failed, not slowly, but with shocking suddenness. Temple fell, crawled a ways, then was still.

It took him minutes to realize the storm no longer buffeted him, more minutes to learn he had managed to crawl into a cave. He had no time to congratulate himself on his good fortune, for something stirred outside.

"I am coming in," the woman called to him from the green murk.

Temple strung an arrow to his bow, pulled the string back and fated the cave's entrance squatting on his heels. "Then your first step shall be your last. I'll shoot to kill." And he meant it.

Silence from outside. Deafening.

Temple felt sweat streaming under his armpits; his hands were clammy, his hands trembled.

"You haven't seen the last of me," the woman promised. After that, Temple knew she was gone. He slept as one dead.

When Temple awoke, bright sunlight filtered in through the foliage outside his cave. Although the ground was a muddy ruin, the storm had stopped. Edging to the mouth of the cave, Temple spread the foliage with his hands, peered cautiously outside. Satisfied, he took his bow and arrows and left the cave, pangs of hunger knotting his stomach painfully.

The cave had been weathered in the side of a short, steep abutment a dozen paces from a gushing, swollen stream. Temple followed the course of the stream as it twisted through the jungle, ranging half a mile from his cave until the water course widened to form a waterhole. All morning Temple waited there, crouching in the grass, until one by one, the forest animals came to drink. He selected a small hare-like thing, notched an arrow to his bow, let it fly.

The animal jumped, collapsed, began to slink away into the undergrowth, dragging the arrow from its hindquarters. Temple darted after it, caught it in his hands and bashed its life out against the bole of a tree. Returning to his cave he found two flinty stones. Then he shredded a fallen branch and nursed the shards dry in the strong sunlight. Soon he made a fire and ate.

IN the days that followed, Temple returned to the waterhole and bagged a new catch every time he ventured forth. Things went so well that he began to range further and further from his cave exploring. Once however, he returned early to the waterhole and found footprints in the soft mud of its banks.

The woman.

That she had been observing him while he had hunted had never occurred to Temple, but now that the proof lay clearly before his eyes, the old feeling of uncertainty came back. And the next day, when he crept stealthily to the waterhole and saw the woman squatting there in the brush, waiting for him, he fled back to his cave.

The thought hit him suddenly. If she were stalking him, why must he flee as from his own shadow? There would be no security for either of them until either one or the other were gone—and gone meant dead. Then Temple would do his own stalking.

For several nights Temple hardly slept. He could have found the waterhole blindfolded merely by following the stream. Each night he would reach the hole and work, digging with a sharp stone, until he had fashioned a pit fully ten feet deep and six feet across. This he covered with branches, twigs, leaves, and finally—dirt.

When he returned in the morning he was satisfied with his work. Unless the woman made a careful study of the area, she would never see the pit. All that day Temple waited with his back to the waterhole, facing the camouflaged pit, the trap he had set, but the woman failed to appear. When she also did not come on the second day, he began to think his plan would not work.

The third day, Temple arrived with the sun, sat as before in the tall grass between the pit and the waterhole and waited. Several paces beyond his hidden trap he could see the tall trees of the jungle with vines and creepers hanging from their branches. At his back, a man's length behind him was the waterhole, its deepest waters no more than waist-high.

Temple waited until the sun stood high in the sky, then was fascinated as a small antelope minced down to the waterhole for a drink. *You'll make a fine breakfast tomorrow, he thought, smiling.*

Something, that strange sixth sense again, made Temple turn around and stand up. He had time for a brief look, a hoarse cry.

The woman had been the cleverer. She had set the final trap. She stood high up on a branch of one of the trees beyond the hidden pit and for an instant Temple saw her fine figure clearly, naked but for the loincloth. Then the soft curves became spring-steel.

The woman arched her body there on the high branch, grasping a stout vine and rocking back with it. Temple raised his bow, set an arrow to let it fly. But by then, the woman was in motion.

Long and lithe and graceful, she swung down on her vine, gathering momentum as she came. Her feet almost brushed the lip of Temple's pit at the lowest arc of her flight, but she clung to the vine and it began to swing up again like a pendulum—toward Temple.

At the last moment he hunched his shoulder and tried to raise his arms for protection. The woman was quicker. She gathered her legs up under her, still clutching the vine with her slim, strong hands. The vine's arc carried her up at him; her knees were at a level with his head and she brought them up savagely, close together striking Temple brutally at the base of his jaw. Temple screamed as his head was jerked back with terrible force.

The bow flew from his fingers and he fell into the waterhole, flat on his back.

Sophia let the vine carry her out over the water, then dropped from it. Waist deep, she waded to where the man lay, unconscious on his back, half in, half out of the shallowest part of the water. She reached him, prodded his chest with her foot. When he did not stir, she rocked her weight down gracefully on her long leg, forcing his head under water. With a haughty smile, she watched the bubbles rise...

In the small room where Temple's body lay in repose on a table the white-smocked doctor looked at the psychotherapist questioningly. "What's happening?"

"Can't tell, doctor. But—"

Suddenly Temple's still body rocked convulsively, his neck stretched, his head shot up and back. Blood trickled from his mouth.

The doctor thrust out expert hands and examined Temple's jaw dexterously.

"Broken?" the psychotherapist demanded in a worried voice.

"No. Dislocated. He looks like he's been hit by a sledgehammer, wherever he is now, whatever's happening. This E.C.R. is the damndest thing."

Temple's still form shuddered convulsively. He began to gasp and cough, obviously fighting for breath. An ugly blue swelling had by now lumped the base of his jaw.

"What's happening?" demanded the psychotherapist.

"I can't be sure," said the doctor, shaking his head. "He seems to have difficulty in breathing...it's as if he were drowning."

"Bad. Anything we can do?"

"No. We wait until this particular sequence ends." The doctor examined Temple again. "If it doesn't end soon, this man will die of asphyxiation."

"Call it off," the psychotherapist pleaded. "If he dies now Earth will be represented by Russia. Call it off!"

Someone entered the room. "I have the authority," he said, selecting a hypodermic from the doctor's rack and piercing the skin of Temple's forearm with it. "This first test has gone far enough. The Russian entry is clearly the winner, but Temple must live if he is to compete in another."

The wracking convulsions that shook Temple's body subsided. He ceased his choking, began to breathe regularly. With grim swiftness, the doctor went to work on Temple's dislocated jaw while the man who had stopped the contest rendered artificial respiration.

The man was Alaric Arkalion.

The Comrade Doctor was exultant. "Jupiter training, comrade, has given us a victory."

"How can you be sure?"

"Our entrant is unharmed, the contest has been called. Wait...she is coming to."

Sophia stretched, rubbed her bruised knees, and sat up.

"What happened, Comrade?" the doctor demanded.

"My knees ache," said Sophia, rubbing them some more. "I—I killed him, I think. Strange, I never dreamed it would be that real."

"In a sense, it was real. If you killed the American, he will stay dead."

"Nothing mattered but that world we were in, a fantastic place. Now I remember everything, all the things I couldn't remember then."

"But your—ah, dream—what happened?"

Sophia rubbed her bruised knees a third time, ruefully. "I knocked him unconscious with these. I forced his head under water and...and drowned him. But...before I could be sure I finished the job—I came back. Funny that I should want to kill him without compunction, without reason." Sophia frowned, sat up. "I don't think I want anymore of this."

The doctor surveyed her coldly. "This is your task on the Stalintrek. This you will do."

"I killed him without a thought."

"Enough. You will rest and get ready for the second contest."

"But if he's dead—"

"Apparently he's not, or we would have been informed, Comrade Petrovitch."

"That is true," agreed the second man, who had remained completely silent until now. "Prepare for another test, Comrade."

Sophia was on the point of arguing again. After all it wasn't fair. If in the dream-worlds that were not dream worlds she was motivated by but one factor and that to destroy the American and if she faced him with the strength of her Jupiter training it would hardly be a contest. And now that she could think of the American without the all-consuming hatred the dream world had fostered in her, she realized he had been a pleasant-looking young man, quite personable, in fact. I could like him, Sophia thought and hoped fervently she had not drowned him. Still, if she had volunteered for the Stalintrek and this was the job they assigned her...

"I need no rest," she told the doctor, hardly trusting herself, for she realized she might change her mind. "I am ready any time you are."

CHAPTER NINE

HIS name was Temple and it was the year 1960. Hectic end of a decade, 1960. Ancient Joe Stalin was still alive, drugged half-senseless against the tortures of an incurable stomach cancer, although the world thought he died in 1953. He would hang on grimly another year and a half, yielding the reins of empire to stout Malenkov who in the space of a few years would lose them to a crafty schoolteacherish whiplash called Beria. 1960—eleventh year of the fantastic Korean situation, in which the Land of the Morning Sun had become, with no pretensions to the contrary, a glorified training camp for the armies of both sides.

The Cold War flared hot in Burma by mid-1960, Indo-China was a Red Fortress and with Tibet hopelessly behind the Iron Curtain, India awoke to the fact that neutrality was an impossibility in the era of pushbuttonry, lending her chaotic bulk to the West. Mao Tse Tung fell before an assassin's bullet in Peking, but a shining new political sewage system cleared the streets of celebration before it fairly got under way. Inside of forty-eight hours, China had a new Red boss—imported from Moscow.

For some reason, it took until 1960 for the first batch of Hiroshima-Nagasaki mutants not to miscarry, and Sunday Supplement editors had a field day with the pathetic little creatures, one of which was born with two heads and actually survived for ten years. In 1960 the first manned spaceship reached Luna, but the public knew nothing of this for another fourteen months. In the United States the increase in taxes and prices was matched everywhere except in the pocketbook of the white-collar worker by an increase in wages. Shortages in all branches of engineering forced the government to subsidize engineering students and exempt them permanently from the draft and the soon-to-be-started Nowhere Journey, while engineers' salaries rose to match those of top business executives.

Big news in the world of sports was the inclusion in the baseball Major Leagues of eight teams from the Pacific Coast, replacing the World Series with what was to become a mathematician's nightmare, the Triangle Game.

But Christopher Temple had his own problems. He had his own life, too, which had nothing to do with the life of the real Christopher Temple, departed thirty-odd years later on the Nowhere Journey. Or rather, this *was* Christopher Temple, living his second E.C.R. Temple who had lost once, and who, if he lost again, would take the dreams and hopes of the Western world down into the dust of defeat with him. But as the fictional (although in a certain sense, real) Christopher Temple of 1960, he knew nothing of this.

The world could go to pot. The world was going to pot, anyway. Temple shuddered as he poured a fourth Canadian, downing it in a tasteless, burning gulp. Temple was a thermonuclear engineer with government subsidized degrees from three universities including the fine new one at Desert Rock. Temple was a thermonuclear engineer with top secret government clearance. Temple was a thermonuclear engineer with more military secrets buzzing around inside his head than in a warehouse of burned Pentagon files.

Temple was also a thermonuclear engineer whose wife spied for the Russians.

HE'D found out quite by accident, not meaning to eavesdrop at all. Returning home early one afternoon because the production engineer called a halt while further research was done on certain unstable isotopes, Temple was surprised to find his wife had a gentleman caller. He heard their voices clearly from where he stood out in the sun-parlor, and for a ridiculous instant he was torn between slinking upstairs and ignoring them altogether or barging into the living room like a high school boy flushed with jealousy. The mature thing to do, of course, was neither, and Temple was on the point of walking politely into the living room, saying hello and waiting for an introduction, when snatches of the conversation stopped him cold.

"Silly Charles! Kit doesn't suspect a thing. I would know."

"How can you be sure?"

"Intuition."

"On a framework of intuition you would place the fate of Red Empire?"

"Empire, Charles?" Temple could picture Lucy's raised eyebrow. He listened now, hardly breathing. For one wild moment he thought he would retreat upstairs and forget the whole thing. Life would be much simpler that way. A meaningless surrender to unreality, however, and it couldn't be done.

"Yes, Empire. Oh, not the land-grabbing, slave-dominating sort of things the Imperialists used to attempt, but a more subtle and hence more enduring empire. Let the world call us Liberator, we shall have Empire."

Lucy laughed, a sound that Temple loved. "You may keep your ideology, Charles. Play with it, bathe in it, get drunk on it or drown yourself in it. I want my money."

"You are frank."

Temple could picture Lucy's shrug. "I am a paid, professional spy. By now you have most of the information you need. I shall have the rest tonight."

"I'll see you in hell first!" Temple cried in rage, stalking into the room and almost smiling in spite of the situation when he realized how melodramatic his words must sound.

"Kit! Kit..." Lucy raised hand to mouth, then backed away flinching as if she had been struck.

"Yeah, Kit. A political cuckold, or does Charles get other services from you as well?"

"Kit, you don't..."

The man named Charles motioned for silence. Dapper, clean-cut, good-looking except for a surly, pouting mouth, he was a head shorter than either Temple or Lucy. "Don't waste your words, Sophia. Temple overheard us."

Sophia? thought Temple. "Sophia?" he said.

Charles nodded coolly. "The real Mrs. Temple was observed, studied, her every habit and whim catalogued by experts. A plastic surgeon, a psychologist, a sociologist, a linguist, a whole battery of experts molded Sophia here into a new Mrs. Temple. I must congratulate them, for you never suspected."

"Lucy?" Temple demanded dully. Reason stood suspended in a limbo of objective acceptance and subjective disbelief.

"Mrs. Temple was eliminated. Regrettable because we don't deal in senseless mayhem, but necessary."

Temple was not aware of leaving limbo until he felt the bruising contact of his knuckles with Charles' jaw. The short man toppled, fell at his feet. "Get up!" Temple cried, then changed his mind and tensed himself to leap upon the prone figure.

"Hold it," Charles told him quietly, wiping blood from his lips with one hand, drawing an automatic from his pocket with the other. "You'd better freeze, Temple. You die if you don't."

TEMPLE froze, watched Charles slither away across the high-piled green carpet until, safely away across the room, he came upright groggily. He turned to the dead Lucy's double. "What do you think, Sophia?"

"I don't know. We could get out of here, probably get along without the final information."

"That isn't what I mean. Naturally, we'll never receive the final facts. I mean, what do you think about Temple?"

Sophia said she didn't know.

"Left alone, he would go to the police. Kidnapped, he would be worse than useless. Harmful, actually, for the authorities would suspect something. Even worse if we killed him. The point is, we don't want the authorities to think Temple gave information to anybody."

"Gave is hardly the word," said Sophia. "I was a good wife, but also a good gleaner. One hundred thousand dollars, Charles."

"You bitch," Temple said.

"Later," Charles told the woman. "The solution is this, Sophia: we must kill Temple, but it must look like suicide."

Sophia frowned in pretty concern. "Do we have to...kill him?"

"What's the matter, my dear? Have you been playing the wifely role too long? If Temple stands in the way of Red Empire, Temple must die."

Temple edged forward.

"Uh-uh," said Charles, "mustn't." he waved the automatic and Temple subsided.

"Is that right?" Sophia demanded. "Well, you listen to me. I have nothing to do with your Red Empire. I fled the Iron Curtain, came here to live voluntarily—"

"Do you really think it was on a voluntary basis that you went? We allowed you to go, Sophia. We encouraged it. That way, the job of our technicians was all the simpler. Whether you like it or not, you have been a cog in the machine of Red Empire."

"I still don't see why he has to die."

"Leave thinking to those who can. You have a smile, a body, a certain way with men. I will think. I think that Temple should die."

"I don't," Sophia said.

"We're delaying needlessly. The man dies." And Charles raised his automatic, sufficiently irked to forget his suicide plan.

A gap of eight or nine feet separated the two men. It might as well have been infinity—and it would be soon, for Temple. He saw Charles' small hand tighten about the automatic, saw the trigger finger grow white. The weapon pointed at a spot just above his navel and briefly he found himself wondering what it would feel like for a slug to rip into his stomach, burning a path back to his spine. He decided to make the gesture at least, if he could do no more. He would jump for Charles.

Sophia beat him to it—and because Lucy was dead and Sophia looked exactly like her and Temple could not quite accept the fact, it seemed the most natural thing in the world. Cat-quick, Sophia leaped upon Charles' back and they went down together in a twisting, thrashing tangle of arms and legs.

Temple did not wait for an invitation. He launched himself down after them, and then things began to happen...fast.

Sophia rolled clear, rose to her hands and knees, panting. Charles sat up cursing, nursing a badly scratched face. Temple hurtled at him, stretched him on his back again, and began to pound hard fists into his face.

Charles did not have the automatic. Neither did Temple.

Something exploded against the back of Temple's head violently, throwing him off Charles and tumbling him over. Dimly he saw Sophia following through, the automatic in her hand, butt foremost. Temple's senses reeled. He tried to rise, succeeded only in a kind of shuddering slither before he subsided. He wavered between consciousness and unconsciousness, heard as in a dream snatches of conversation.

"Shoot him shoot him!"

"Shut up I have...gun...go to hell."

"...kill...only way."

"My way is different...out of here...discuss later."

"...feel..."

"I said...out of here..."

The voices became a meaningless liquid torrent cascading into a black pit.

NOW Temple sat with a water glass a third full of Canadian in his hand, every once in a while reaching up gingerly to explore the bruised swelling on his head, the blood-matted hair that covered it. To be a cuckold was one thing, but to be the naive, political pawn sort of cuckold who is not a cuckold at all, he told himself, is far worse. To live with his woman, eat the meals she cooked for him, talk to her, think she understood him, sympathize with him, to make love to her with passion while she responds with play-acting for a hundred thousand dollar salary was suddenly the most emasculating thing in the world for Temple. He had not thought to ask how long it had been going on. Better, perhaps, if he never knew. And somewhere lost in the maze of his thoughts was the grimmest, bleakest reality of them all: Lucy was dead. Lucy—dead. But where did Lucy leave off, where did Sophia begin? Was Lucy dead that night they returned more than a little drunk from the Chamber's party, that night they danced in the living room until dawn obscured the stars and he carried Lucy upstairs. Lucy or Sophia? And the day they motored to the lake, their secret lake, hardly more than a dammed, widened stream and dreamed of the things they could do when the Cold War ended? Lucy—or Sophia? Had he ever noticed a difference in the way Lucy-Sophia cooked, in the way she spoke, the way she let him make love to her? He thought himself into a man-sized headache and found no answers. This way at least the loss of his wife was not as traumatic as it might have been. He knew not when she died or how and, in fact, Lucy-Sophia seemed so much like the real thing that he did not know where he could stop loving and start hating.

And the girl, the Russian girl, had saved his life. Why? He couldn't answer that one either, unless if it were as Charles suggested: Sophia had studied Lucy so carefully, had learned her likes and dislikes, her wants and desires, had memorized and practiced every quirk of her character to such an extent that Sophia was Lucy in essence.

Which, Temple thought, would make it all the harder to seek out Sophia and kill her.

That was the answer, the only answer. Temple felt a dull ache where his heart should have been, a pressure, a pounding, an unpleasant, unfamiliar lack of feeling. If he took his story to the FBI he had no doubt that Charles, Sophia and whoever else worked this thing with them would be caught, but he, Temple, would find himself with a lifelong, unslakable emotional thirst. He had to quench it now and then feel sorry so that he might heal. He had to quench it with Sophia's blood...alone.

HE found her a week later at their lake. He had looked everywhere and had about given up, almost, in fact, ready to turn his story over to the police. But he had to think and their lake was the place for that.

Apparently Sophia had the same idea. Temple parked on the highway half a mile from their lake, made his way slowly through the woods, golden dappled with sunlight. He heard the waters gushing merrily, heard the sounds of some small animal rushing off through the woods. He saw Sophia.

She lay on their sunning rock in shorts and halter, completely relaxed, an opened magazine face down on the rock beside her, a pair of sunglasses next to it. She had one knee up, one leg stretched out, one forearm shielding her eyes from the sun, one arm down at her side. Seeing her thus, Temple felt the pressure of his automatic in its holster under his arm. He could draw it out, kill her before she was aware of his presence. Would that make him feel better? Five minutes ago, he would have said yes. Now he hesitated. Kill *her*...who seemed as completely Lucy as he was Temple? Send a bullet ripping through the body that he had known and loved, or the body that had seemed so much like it he had failed to tell the difference?

Murder—Lucy?

"No," he said aloud. "Her name is Sophia."

The girl sat up, startled. "Kit," she said.

"Lucy."

"You can't make up your mind, either." she smiled just like Lucy.

Dumbly, he sat down next to her on the rock. Strong sunlight had brought a fine dew of perspiration to the bronzed skin of her face. She got a pack of cigarettes out from under the magazine, lit one, offered it to Temple, lit another and smoked it. "Where do we go from here?" she wanted to know.

"I—"

"You came to kill me, didn't you? Is that the only way you can ever feel better, Kit?"

"I—" He was going to deny it, then think of something else to say.

"Don't deny it...please." she reached in under his jacket, withdrawing her hand with the snub-nosed automatic in it.

"Here," she said, giving it to him.

He took the gun, hefted it, let it fall, clattering, on the rock.

"Listen," she said. "I could have told you I was Lucy. If I said now that I am Lucy and if I kept on saying it, you'd believe me. You'd believe me because you'd want to."

"Well," said Temple.

"I am not Lucy. Lucy is dead. But...but I was Lucy in everything but being Lucy. I thought her thoughts, dreamed her dreams, loved her loves."

"You killed her."

"No. I had nothing to do with that. She was killed, yes. Not by me. Kit, if I asked you when Lucy stopped, and...when I began, could you tell me?"

He had often thought about that. "No," he said truthfully. "You're as much my wife as—she was."

SHE clutched at his hand impulsively. Then, when he failed to respond, she withdrew her own hand. "Then—then I am Lucy. If I am Lucy in every way, Lucy never died."

"You betrayed me. You stood by while murder was committed. You are guilty of espionage."

"Lucy loved you. I am Lucy..."

"...Betrayed me..."

"For a hundred thousand dollars. For the chance to live a normal life, for the chance to forget Leningrad in the wintertime, watery potato soup, rags for clothing, swaggering commissars, poverty, disease. Do you think I realized I could fall in love with you so completely? If I did, don't you think that would have changed things? I am not Sophia, Kit. I was, but I am not. They made me Lucy. Lucy can't be dead, not if I'm her in every way."

"What can we do?"

"I—don't know. I only want to be your wife..."

"Well, then tell me," he said bitterly. "Shall I go back to the plant and continue working, knowing all the time that our most closely guarded secret is in Russian hands and that my wife is responsible?" He laughed. "Shall I do that?"

"Your secrets never went anywhere."

"Shall I…what?"

"Your secrets never went anywhere. Charles is dead. I have destroyed all that we took. I am not Russian any longer. American. They made me American. They made me Lucy. I want to go right on being Lucy, your wife."

Temple said nothing for a long time. He realized now he could not kill her. But everything else she suggested… "Tell me," he said. "Tell me, how long have you been Lucy? You've got to tell me that."

"How long have we been married?"

"You know how long. Three years."

Sophia crushed her cigarette out on the rock, wiped perspiration (tears?) from her cheek with the back of her hand. "You have never known anyone but me in your marriage bed, Kit."

"You—you're lying."

"No. They did what they did on the eve of your marriage. I have been your wife for as long as you have had one."

Temple's head whirled. It had been a quick courtship. He had known Lucy only two weeks in those hectic postgraduate days of 1957. But for fourteen brief days, it was Sophia he had known all along.

"Sophia, I—"

"There is no Sophia, not any more."

He had hardly known Lucy, the real Lucy. This girl here was his wife, always had been. Had the first fourteen days with Lucy been anything but a dream? He was sorry Lucy had died—but the Lucy he had thought dead was Sophia, very much alive.

He took her in his arms, almost crushing her. He held her that way, kissed her savagely, letting passion of a different sort take the place of murder.

This is my woman, he thought, and awoke on his white pallet in Nowhere.

"I AM awake," said Temple.

"We see that. You shouldn't be."

"No?"

"No. There is one more dream."

Temple dozed restfully but was soon aware of a commotion. Strangely, he did not care. He was too tired to open his eyes, anyway. Let whatever was going to happen, happen. He wanted his sleep.

But the voice persisted.

"This is highly irregular. You came in here once and—"

"I did you a favor, didn't I?" (That voice is familiar, Temple thought.)

"Well, yes. But what now?"

"Temple's record is now one and one. In the second sequence he was the victor. The Soviet entry had to extract certain information from him and turn it over to her people. She extracted the information well enough but somehow Temple made her change her mind. The information never went anyplace. How Temple managed to play counterspy I don't know, but he played it and won."

"That's fine. But what do you want?"

"The final K.C.R. is critical." (The voice was Arkalion's!) "How critical, I can't tell you. Sufficient though, if you know that you lose no matter how Temple fares. If the Russian woman defeats Temple, you lose."

"Naturally."

"Let me finish. If Temple defeats the Russian woman, you also lose. Either way, Earth is the loser. I haven't time to explain what you wouldn't understand anyway. Will you cooperate?"

"Umm-mm. You did save Temple's life. Umm-mm, yes. All right."

"The third dream sequence is the wrong dream, the wrong contest with the wrong antagonist at the wrong time, when a far more important contest is brewing…with the fate of Earth as a reward for the victor."

"What do you propose?"

"I will arrange Temple's final dream. But if he disappears from this room, don't be alarmed. It's a dream of a different sort. Temple won't know it until the dream progresses, you won't know it until everything is concluded, but Temple will fight for a slave or a free Earth."

"Can't you tell us more?"

"There is no time, except to say that along with the rest of the Galaxy, you've been duped. The Nowhere Journey is a grim, tragic farce.

"Awaken, Kit!"

Temple awoke into what he thought was the third and final dream. Strange, because this time he knew where he was and why. He knew also that he was dreaming—and even remembered vividly the other two dreams.

"STEALTH," said Arkalion, and led Temple through long, white-walled corridors. They finally came to a partially open door and paused there. Peering within, Temple saw a room much like the one he had left, with two white-gowned figures standing anxiously over a table. And prone on the table was Sophia, whom Temple had loved short moments before, in his second dream. Moments? Years. (Never, except in a dream.)

"She's lovely," Arkalion whispered.

"I know." Like himself, Sophia was garbed in a loose

jumper and slacks.

"Stealth," said Arkalion again. "Haste." Arkalion disappeared.

"Well," Temple told himself. "What now? At least in the other dreams I was thrust so completely into things, I knew what to do." he rubbed his jaw grimly. "Not that it did much good the first time."

Temple poked the partially ajar door with his foot, pushing it open. The two white-smocked figures had their backs to him, leaned intently over the table and Sophia. Without knowing what motivated him, Temple leaped into the room, grasped the nearer figure's arm, whirled him around. Startled confusion began to alter the man's coarse features, but his face went slack when Temple's fist struck his jaw with terrible strength. The man collapsed.

The second man turned, mouthing a stream of what must have been Russian invective. He parried Temple's quick blow with his left hand, crossing his own right fist to Temple's face and almost ending the fight as quickly as it had started. Temple went down in a heap and was vaguely aware of the Russian's booted foot hovering over his face. He reached out, grabbed the boot with both hands, and twisted. The man screamed and fell. Then they were rolling over and over, striking each other with fists, knees, elbows, gouging, butting, cursing. Temple found the Russian's throat, closed his hands around it, and applied pressure. Fists pounded his face, nails raked him, but slowly he succeeded in throttling the Russian. When Temple got to his feet, trembling, the Russian stared blankly at the ceiling. He would go on staring that way until someone shut his eyes.

Not questioning the incomprehensible, Temple knew he had done what he must. Hardly seeking for the motive he could not find, he lifted the unconscious Sophia off the table, slung her long form across his shoulder, and plodded with her from the room. Arkalion had said haste. He would hurry.

He next was aware of a spaceship. Remembering no time lag, he simply stood in the ship with Arkalion. And Sophia.

HE knew it was a spaceship because he had been in one before and although the sensation of weightlessness was not present, they were in deep space. Stars you never see through an obscuring atmosphere hung suspended in the viewports. Cold bright, not flickering against the plush blackness of deep space, phalanxes and legions of stars without numbers, in such wild profusion that space actually seemed three dimensional.

"This is a different sort of dream," said Sophia in English. "I remember. I remember everything. Kit—"

"Hello." he felt strangely shy, became mildly angry when Arkalion hardly tried to suppress a slight snicker. "Well, that second dream wasn't our idea," Temple protested. "Once there, we acted...and—"

"And..." said Sophia.

"And nothing," Arkalion told them. "You haven't time. This is a spaceship, not like the slow, bumbling crafts your people use to reach Mars or Jupiter."

"Our people?" Temple demanded. "Not yours?"

"Will you let me finish? Light is a laggard crawler by comparison with the drive propelling this ship. Temple, Sophia, we are leaving your Galaxy altogether."

"Is that a fact?" said Sophia, her Jupiter-found knowledge telling her they were traveling an unthinkable distance. "For some final contest between us, no doubt, to decide whether the U.S.S.R. or the U.S. represents Earth? Kit, I—I—love you, but..."

"But Russia is more important, huh?"

"No. I didn't say that. All my training has been along

those lines, though, and even if I'm aware it is indoctrination, the fact still remains. If your country is truly better, but if I have seen your country only through the eyes of Pravda, how can I...I don't know, Kit. Let me think."

"You needn't," said Arkalion, smiling. "If the two of you would let me get on with it you'd see this particular train of thought is meaningless, quite meaningless." Arkalion cleared his throat. "Strange, but I have much the same problem as Sophia. My indoctrination was far more subtle though. Far more convincing, based upon eons of propaganda methods. Temple, Sophia, those who initiated the Nowhere Journey for hundreds of worlds of your galaxy did so with a purpose."

"I know. To decide who gets their vast knowledge."

"Wrong. To find suitable hosts in a one-way relationship that is hardly symbiosis, but rather, a relationship that is really out and out parasitism."

"What?"

And Sophia: "What are you talking about?"

"The sick, decadent, tired old creatures you consider your superiors. Parasites. They need hosts in order to survive. Their old hosts have been milked dry, have become too highly specialized, are now incapable physically or emotionally of meeting a wide variety of environmental challenges. The Nowhere Journey is to find a suitable new host. They have found one. You of Earth."

"I don't understand," Temple said, remembering the glowing accounts of the 'superboys' he had been given by his brother Jason. "I just don't get it. How can we be duped like that? Wouldn't someone have figured it out? And if they have all the power everyone says, there isn't much we can do about it, anyway."

Arkalion scowled darkly. "Then write Earth's obituary. You'll need one."

"Go ahead," Sophia told Arkalion. "There's more you

want to say."

"All right. Temple's thought is correct. They have tremendous power. That is why you could be duped so readily. But their power is not concentrated here. These go-much-faster-than-light ships are an extreme rarity, for the power-drive no longer exists. Five ships in all, I believe. Hardly enough to invade a planet, even for them. It takes them thousands of years to get here otherwise. Thousands. Just as it took me, when I came to Mars and Earth in the first place."

"What?" cried Temple. "You..."

"I am one of them. Correct. I suppose you would call me a subversive, but I have made up my mind. Parasitism is unsatisfactory, when the Maker got us started on symbiosis. Somewhere along the line, evolution took a wrong turn. We are—monsters."

"What do you look like?" Sophia demanded while Temple stood there shaking his head and muttering to himself.

"YOU couldn't see me, I am afraid. I was the representative here to see how things were going, and when my people found you of the Earth divided yourselves into two camps they realized they had been considering your abilities in halves. Put together, you are probably the top culture of your galaxy."

"So, we win," said Temple.

"Right and wrong. You lose. Earthmen will become hosts. Know what a backseat driver is, Temple? You would be a back seat driver in your own body. Thinking, feeling, wanting to make decisions, but unable to. Eating when the parasite wants to, sleeping at his command, fighting, loving, living as he wills it. And perishing when he wants a new garment. Oh, they offer something in return. Their culture, their way of life, their scientific, economic, social system. It's good, too. But not worth it. Did you know that their economic struggle between democratic capitalism and totalitarian communism ended almost half a million years ago? What they have now is a system you couldn't even understand."

"Well," Temple mused, "even if everything you said were true—"

"Don't tell me you don't believe me?"

"If it were true and we wanted to do something about it, what could we do?"

"Now, nothing. Nothing but delay things by striking swiftly and letting fifty centuries of time perform your rearguard action. Destroy the one means your enemy has of reaching Earth within foreseeable time and you have destroyed his power to invade for a hundred centuries. He can still reach Earth, but the same way you journeyed to Nowhere. Ten thousand years of space travel in suspended animation. You saw me that way once, Temple, and wondered. You thought I was dead, but that is another story.

"Anyway, let my people invade your planet, ten thousand years hence. If Earth takes the right direction, if democracy and free thought and individual enterprise win over totalitarian standardization as I think they will, your people will be more than a match for the decadent parasites who may or may not have sufficient initiative to cross space the slow way and attempt invasion in ten thousand years."

"Ten thousand?" said Temple.

"Five from Earth to Nowhere. The distance to my home is far greater, but the rate of travel can be increased. Ten thousand years."

"Tell me," Temple demanded abruptly, "is this a dream?"

Arkalion smiled. "Yes and no. It is not a dream like the others because I assure you your bodies are not now resting on a pair of identical white tables. Still in the other dreams physical things could happen to you, while now you'll find you can do things as in a dream. For example, neither one of you knows the intricacies of a spaceship, yet if you are to save your planet, you must know the operation of the most intricate of all space ships, a giant space station."

"Then we're not dreaming?" asked Temple.

"I never said that. Consider this sequence of events about half way between the dream stage you have already seen and reality itself. Remember this, you'll have to work together; you'll have to function like machines. You will be handling totally alien equipment with only the sort of knowledge that can be played into your brains to guide you."

Sophia sighed. "Being an American, Kit is too much of an individual to help in such a situation."

Temple snorted. "Being a cog in a simple, state-wide machine is one thing—orienting yourself in a totally new situation is another."

"Yes, well—"

"See?" Arkalion cautioned. "See? Already you are arguing, but you must work together completely, with not the slightest conflict between, you. As it is, you hardly have a chance."

"What about you?" said Sophia practically. "Can't you help?"

ARKALION shook his head. "No. While I'd like to see you come out of this thing on top, I would not like to sacrifice my life for it—which is exactly what I'd do if I remained with you and you lost.

"So, let's get down to detail. Imagine space being folded, imagine your time sense slowing, imagine a new dimension that negates the need for extensive linear travel, imagine anything you want—but we are in the process of moving nine hundred thousand light years through deep space. There is a great galaxy at that distance, almost a twin of your Milky Way. You call it the Andromeda Nebula. Closer to your own system are the two Magellanic Clouds, so called, something else which you table NGC 6822, and finally the Triangulum Galaxy. All have billions of stars, but none of the stars have life. To find life outside your galaxy you must seek it across almost a million light years. My people live in Andromeda.

"Guarding the flank of their galaxy and speeding through inter-galactic space at many light-years per minute is what you might call a space station—but on a scale you've never dreamed of. Five of your miles in diameter, it is a fortress of terrible strength, a storehouse of half a million years of weapon development. It has been arranged that the one man running this station—"

"Just one?" Temple asked.

"Yes. You will see why when you get there. It has been arranged that he will leave, ostensibly on a scouting expedition. You see, I am not alone in this venture. At any rate, he will report that the space station has been taken—as indeed it will be, by the two of you. The only ships capable of overtaking your station in its flight will be the only ships capable of reaching your galaxy before cultural development gives you a chance to survive. They will attack you. You will destroy them—or be destroyed yourselves. Any questions?"

The whole thing sounded fantastic to Temple. Could the fate of all Earth rest on their shoulders in a totally alien environment? Could they be expected to win? Temple had no reason to doubt the former, as wild as it sounded. As for the latter, all he could do was hope. "Tell me," he said, "how will we learn the use of all the weapons you claim are at our disposal?"

"Can you answer that for him, Sophia?" Arkalion wanted to know.

"Umm, I think so. The same way I had all sorts of culture

crammed into me on Jupiter."

"Precisely. Only take it from me our refinement is far better, and the amount you have to learn actually is less."

"What I'd like to know—" Sophia began.

"Forget it. I want some sleep and you'll learn everything that's necessary at the space station."

And after that, ply Arkalion as they would with questions, he slumped down in his chair and rested. Temple could suddenly understand and appreciate. He felt like curling up into a tight little ball himself and sleeping until everything was over, one way or the other.

CHAPTER TEN

"IT'S all so big! So incredible! We'll never understand it! Never..."

"Relax, Sophia. Arkalion said—"

"I know what Arkalion said, but we haven't learned anything yet."

Hours before, Arkalion had landed them on the space station, a gleaming, five-mile in diameter globe, and had quickly departed. Soon after that they had found themselves in a veritable labyrinth of tunnels, passageways, vaults. Occasionally they passed a great glowing screen, and always the view of space was the same. Like a magnificent, elongated shield, sparkling with a million million points of light, pale gold, burnished copper, blue of glacial ice and silver white, the Andromeda Galaxy spanned space from upper right to lower left. Off at the lower right hand corner they could see their space station; apparently the viewer itself stood far removed in space, projecting its images here at the globe.

Awed the first time they had seen one of the screens, Temple said, "All the poets who ever wrote a line would have given half their lives to see this as we see it now."

"And all the writers, musicians, artists..."

"Anyone who ever thought creatively, Sophia. How can you say it's breathtaking or anything like that when words weren't ever spoken that can..."

"Let's not go poetic just yet," Sophia admonished him with a smile. "We'd better get squared away here, as the expression goes, before it's too late."

"Yes...hello, what's this?" A door irised open for them in

a solid wall of metal. Irised was the only word Temple could think of, for a tiny round hole appeared in the wall spreading evenly in all directions with a slow, uniform, almost liquid motion. When it was large enough to walk through, they entered a completely bare room and Temple whirled in time to see the entrance irising shut.

"Something smells," said Sophia, sniffing at the air.

Sweet and cloying, the odor grew stronger. Temple may have heard a faint hissing sound. "I'm getting sleepy," he said.

Nodding, Sophia ran, banged on the wall where the door had opened so suddenly, then closed. No response. "Is it a trap?"

"By whom? For what?" Temple found it difficult to keep his eyes from dosing. "Fight it if you want, Sophia. I'm going to sleep." And he squatted in the center of the floor, staring vacantly at the bare wall.

Just as Temple was drifting off into a dream about complex machinery he did not yet understand but realized he soon would, Sophia joined him the hard way, collapsing alongside of him, unconscious and sprawling gracelessly on the floor.

Temple slept.

"SLEEPY-HEAD, get up."

Sophia stirred as he spoke and shook her. She yawned, stretched, smiled up at him lazily.

"How do you feel now?"

"Hungry, Kit."

"That's a point. It's all right now, though. I know exactly where the food concentrates are kept. Three levels below us, second segment of the wall. You can make those queer doors iris by pressing the wall twice, with about a one second interval."

They found the food compartment, discovered row on row of cans, boxes, jars. Temple opened one of the cans, gazed in disappointment on a sorry looking thing the size of his thumb. Brown, shriveled, dry and almost flaky, it might have been a bird.

Sophia turned up her nose. "If that's the best this place has to offer, I'm not so hungry anymore."

Suddenly, she gaped. So did Temple. A savory odor attracted their attention, steam rising from the small can added to their interest. Amazing things happened to the withered scrap of food on exposure to the air. Temple barely had time to extract it from the can, burning his fingers in the process, when it became twice the can's size. It grew and by the time it finished, it was as savory looking a five-pound fowl as Temple had ever seen. Roasted, steaming hot, ready to eat.

They tore into it with savage gusto.

"Stephanie should see me now," Temple found himself saying and regretted it.

"Stephanie? Who's that?"

"A girl."

"Your girl?"

"What's the difference? She's a million light years and fifty centuries away."

"Answer me."

"Yes," said Temple, wishing he could change the subject. "My girl." he hadn't thought of Stephanie in a long time, perhaps because it was meaningless to think of someone dead fifty centuries. Now that the thoughts had been stirred within him, though, he found them poignantly pleasant.

"Your girl...and you would marry her if you could?"

He had grown attached to Sophia, not in reality, but in the second of their dream worlds. He wished the memory of the dream had not lingered, for it disturbed him. In it he had loved Sophia as much as he now loved Stephanie, although the one was obtainable and the other was a five-thousand-year pinch of dust. And how much of the dream lingered with him, in his head and his heart?

"Let's forget about it," Temple suggested.

"No. If she were here today and if everything were normal, would you marry her?"

"Why talk about what can't be?"

"I want to know, that's why."

"All right. Yes, I would. I would marry Stephanie."

"Oh," said Sophia. "Then what happened in the dream meant...nothing."

"We were two different people," Temple said coolly, then wished he hadn't for it was only half-true. He remembered everything about the dream-which-was-more-than-a-dream vividly. He had been far more intimate with Sophia, and over a longer period of time, than he had ever been with Stephanie. And even if Stephanie appeared impossibly on the spot and he spent the rest of his life as her husband, still he would never forget his dream-life with Sophia. In time he could let himself tell her that. But not now; now the best thing he could do would be to change the subject.

"I see," Sophia answered him coldly.

"No, you don't. Maybe some day you will."

"There's nothing but what you told me. I see."

"No...forget it," he told her wearily.

"Of course. It was only a dream anyway. The dream before that I almost killed you out of hatred anyway. Love and hate, I guess they neutralize. We're just a couple of people who have to do a job together, that's all."

"For gosh sakes, Sophia! That isn't true. I loved Stephanie. I still would, were Stephanie alive. But she's— she's about as accessible as the Queen of Sheba."

"So? There's an American expression—you're carrying a

torch."

Probably, Temple realized, it was true. But what did all of that have to do with Sophia? If he and Sophia…if they…would it be fair to Sophia? It would be exactly as if a widower remarried, with the memory of his first wife set aside in his heart…no, different, for he had never wed Stephanie, and always in him would be the desire for what had never been.

"Let's talk about it some other time," Temple almost pleaded, wanting the respite for himself as much as for Sophia.

"No. We don't have to talk about it ever. I won't be second best, Kit. Let's forget all about it and do our job. I—I'm sorry I brought the whole thing up."

Temple felt like an unspeakable heel. And, anyway, the whole thing wasn't resolved in his mind. But they couldn't just let it go at that, not in case something happened when the ships came and one or both of them perished. Awkwardly, for now he felt self-conscious about everything, he got his arms about Sophia, drew her to him, placed his lips to hers.

That was as far as he got. She wrenched free, shoved clear of him. "If you try that again, you will have another dislocated jaw."

Temple shrugged wearily. If anything were to be resolved between them, it would be later.

When the ships came moments afterwards—seven, not the five Arkalion predicted—they were completely unprepared.

TEMPLE spotted them first on one of the viewing screens, half way between the receiver and the space station itself, silhouetted against the elongated shield of Andromeda. They soared out of the picture, appeared again minutes later, zooming in from the other direction in two flights of four ships and three.

"Come on!" Sophia cried over her shoulder, irising the door and plunging from the room. Temple followed at her heels but her Jupiter trained muscles pushed her lithe legs in long, powerful strides and soon she outdistanced him. By the time he reached the armaments vault, breathless, she was seated at the single gun-emplacement, her fingers on the controls.

"Watch the viewing screen and tell me how we're doing," Sophia told him, not taking her eyes from the dials and levers.

Temple watched, fascinated, saw a thin pencil of radiant energy leap out into space, missing one of the ships by what looked like a scant few miles. He called the corrective azimuth to her, hardly surprised by the way his mind had absorbed and now could use its newfound knowledge.

Temple understood and yet did not understand. For example, he knew the station had but one gun and Sophia sat at it now, yet in certain ways it didn't make sense. Could it cover all sectors of space? His mind supplied the answer although he had not been aware of the knowledge an instant before: yes. The space station did not merely rotate. Its surface was a spherical projection of a moving Moebius strip and although he tried to envision the concept, he failed. The weapon could be fired at any given point in space at twenty-second intervals, covering every other conceivable point in the ensuing time.

Sophia was firing again and Temple watched the thin beam leap across space. "Hit!" he roared. "Hit!"

Something flashed at the front end of the lead ship. The light blinded him, but when he could see again only six ships remained in space—casting perfect shadows on the Andromeda Galaxy! The source of light, Temple realized triumphantly, was out of range, but he could picture it—a glowing derelict of a ship, spewing heat, light and radioactivity into the void.

"One down," Sophia called. "Six to go. I like your American expressions. Like sitting ducks—"

She did not finish. Abruptly, light flared all around them. Something shrieked in Temple's ears. The vault shuddered, shook. Girders clattered to the floor, stove it in, revealing black rock. Sophia was thrown back from the single gun, crashing against the wall, flipping in air and landing on her stomach.

Temple ran to her, turned her over. Blood smeared her face, trickled from her lips. Although she did not move, she wasn't dead. Temple half dragged, half carried her from the vault into an adjoining room. He stretched her out comfortably as he could on the floor, then ran back into the vault.

Molten metal had collected in one corner of the room and crept sluggishly toward him across the floor, heating it white-hot. He skirted it, climbed over a twisted girder, pushed his way past other debris, and found himself at the gun emplacement.

"How dumb can I get?" Temple said aloud. "Sophia ran to the gun, must have assumed I set up the shields." Again, it was an item of information stored in his mind by the wisdom of the space station. Protective shields made it impossible for anything but a direct hit on the emplacement to do them any harm, only Temple had never set the shields in place. He did so now, merely by tripping a series of levers, but glancing at a dial to his left he realized with alarm that the damage possibly had already been done. The needle, which measured lethal radiation, hovered half way between negative and the critical area marked in red and, even as Temple watched it, crept closer to the red.

HOW much time did he have? Temple could not be sure, bent grimly over the weapon. It was completely unfamiliar to his mind, completely unfamiliar to his fingers. He toyed with it, released a blast of radiant energy, whirled to face the viewing screen. The beam streaked out into the void, clearly hundreds of miles from its objective.

Cursing, Temple tried again, scoring a near miss. The ships were trading a steady stream of fire with him now, but with the shielding up it was harmless, striking and then bouncing back into space. Temple scored his first hit five minutes after sitting down at the gun. He whooped triumphantly and fired again. Five ships left.

But the dial indicated an increase in radioactivity as newly created neutrons spread their poison like a cancer. Behind Temple, the vault was a shambles. The pool of molten metal had increased in size, almost cutting off any possibility of escape. He could jump it now, Temple realized, but it might grow larger. Consolidating its gains now, it had sheared a pit in the floor, and had commenced vaporizing the rock below it, hissing and lapping with white-hot insistence.

Something boomed, grated, boomed again and Temple watched another girder bounce off the floor, dip one end into the molten pool, and clatter out a stub. Apparently the damage was extensive; a structural weakness threatened to make the entire ceiling go.

Temple fired again, got another ship. He could almost feel death breathing on his shoulder, in no great hurry but sure of its prize. He fired the weapon.

If one ship remained when they could no longer use the gun, they would have failed. One ship might make the difference for Earth. One...

Three left. Two.

They raked the space station with blast after blast— futilely. They spun and twisted and streaked by, offering poor targets. Temple waited his chance…and glanced at the dial that measured radioactivity. He yelped and stood up. The needle had encroached upon the red area. Death to remain where he was more than a moment or two. Not quick death, but rather slow and lingering. He could do what he had to, then perish hours later. His life—for Earth? If Arkalion had known all the answers, and if he could get both ships and if there weren't another alternative for the aliens, the parasites… Temple stabbed out with his pencil beam, caught the sixth ship, then saw the needle dip completely into the red. He got up trembling, stepped back, half tripped on the stump of a girder as his eyes strayed in fascination to the viewing screen. The seventh ship was out of range, hovering off in the void somewhere, awaiting its chance. If Temple left the gun the ship would come in close enough to hit the emplacement despite its protective shielding. Well, it was suicide to remain there—especially when the ship wasn't even in view.

Temple leaped over the molten pool and left the vault.

HE found Sophia stirring, sitting up.

"What hit me?" she said, and laughed. "Something seems to have gone wrong, Kit…what…?"

"It's all right now," he told her, lying.

"You look pale."

"You got one. I got five. One ship to go."

"What are you waiting for?" And Sophia sprang to her feet, heading for the vault.

"Hold it!" Temple snapped. "Don't go in there."

"Why not. I'll get the last ship and—"

"Don't go in there!" Temple tugged at her arm, pulled her away from the vault and its broken door that would not iris closed any more.

"What's the matter, Kit?" "I—I want to finish the last one

myself, that's all."

Sophia got herself loose, reached the circular doorway, peered inside. "Like Dante's Inferno," she said. "You told me nothing was the matter. Well, we can get through to the emplacement, Kit."

"No." And again he stopped her. At least he had lived in freedom all his life and although he was still young and did not want to die, Sophia had never known freedom until now and it wouldn't be right if she perished without savoring its fruits. He had a love, dust fifty centuries, he had his past and his memories. Sophia had only the future. Clearly, if someone had to yield life, Temple would do it.

"It's worse than it looks," he told her quietly, drawing her hack from the door again. He explained what had happened, told her the radioactivity had not quite reached critical point—which was a lie. "So," he concluded, "we're wasting time. If I rush in there, fire, and rush right out everything will be fine."

"Then let me. I'm quicker than you."

"No. I—I'm more familiar with the gun." Dying would not be too bad, if he went with reasonable certainty he had saved the Earth. No man ever died so importantly, Temple thought briefly, then felt cold fear when he realized it would be dying just the same. He fought it down, said: "I'll be right back."

Sophia looked at him, smiling vaguely. "Then you insist on doing it?"

When he nodded she told him, "Then—kiss me. Kiss me now, Kit—in case something…"

Fiercely, he swept her to him, bruising her lips with his. "Sophia, Sophia…"

At last, she drew back. "Kit," she said, smiling demurely. She took his right hand in her left, held it, squeezed it. Her own right hand she suddenly brought up from her waist, fist clenched, driving it against his jaw.

Temple fell, half stunned by the blow, at her feet. For the space of a single heartbeat he watched her move slowly toward the round doorway, then he had clambered to his feet, running after her. He got his arms on her shoulders, yanked at her.

When she turned he saw she was crying. "I—I'm sorry, Kit. You couldn't fool me about...Stephanie. You can't fool me about this." she had more leverage this time. She stepped back, bringing her small, hard fist up from her knees. It struck Temple squarely at the point of the jaw, with the strength of Jovian-trained muscle behind it. Temple's feet left the floor and he landed with a thud on his back. His last thought of Sophia—or of anything, for a while—made him smile faintly as he lost consciousness. For a kiss she had promised him another dislocated jaw, and she had kept her promise...

*　　*　　*

Later, how much later he did not know, something soft cushioned his head. He opened his eyes, stared through swirling, spinning murk. He focused, saw Arkalion. No— two Arkalions standing off at a distance, watching him. He squirmed, knew his head was cushioned in a woman's lap. He sighed, tried to sit up and failed. Soft hands caressed his forehead, his cheeks. A face swam into vision, but mistily. "Sophia," he murmured. His vision cleared.

It was Stephanie.

"IT'S over," said Arkalion. "We're on our way back to Earth, Kit."

"But the ships—"

"All destroyed. If my people want to come here in ten

thousand years, let them try. I have a hunch you of Earth will be ready for them."

"It took us five thousand to reach Nowhere," Temple mused. "It will take us five thousand to return. We'll come barely in time to warn Earth—"

"Wrong," said Arkalion. "I still have my ship. We're in it now, so you'll reach Earth with almost fifty centuries to spare. Why don't you forget about it, though? If human progress for the next five thousand years matches what has been happening for the last five, the parasites won't stand a chance."

"Earth—five thousand years in the future," Stephanie said dreamily. "I wonder what it will be like...don't be so startled, Kit. I was a pilot study on the Nowhere journey. If I made it successfully, other women would have been sent. But now there won't be any need."

"I wouldn't be too sure of that," said the real Alaric Arkalion III. "I suspect a lot of people are going to feel just like me. Why not go out and colonize space. We can do it. Wonderful to have a frontier again...why, a dozen billionaires will appear for every one like my father. Good for the economy."

"So, if we don't like Earth," said Stephanie, "we can always go out."

"I have a strong suspicion you will like it," said Arkalion's double.

Alaric III grinned. "What about you, bud? I don't want a twin brother hanging around all the time."

Arkalion grinned back at him. "What do you want me to do, young man? I've forsaken my people. This is now my body. Tell you what, I promise to be always on a different continent. Earth isn't so small that I'll get in your hair."

Temple sat up, felt the bandages on his jaw. He smiled at Stephanie, told her he loved her and meant it. It was exactly as if she had returned from the grave and in his first exultation he hadn't even thought of Sophia, who had perished all alone in the depths of space that a world might live...

He turned to Arkalion. "Sophia?"

"We found her dead, Kit. But smiling, as if everything was worth it."

"It should have been me."

"Whoever Sophia was," said Stephanie, "she must have been a wonderful woman, because when you got up, when you came to, her name was..."

"Forget it," said Temple. "Sophia and I have a very strange relationship and..."

"All right, you said forget it. Forget it." Stephanie smiled down at him. "I love you so much there isn't even room for jealousy...ummm...Kit..."

"Break up that clinch," ordered Arkalion. "We're making one more stop at Nowhere to pick up anyone who wants to return to Earth. Some of 'em probably won't but those who do are welcome..."

"Jason will stay," Temple predicted. "He'll be a leader out among the stars."

"Then he'll have to climb over my back," Alaric III predicted happily, his eyes on the viewport hungrily.

Temple's jaw throbbed. He was tired and sleepy. But satisfied, Sophia had died and for that he was sad, but there would always be a place deep in his heart for the memory of her: delicious, somehow exotic, not a love the way Stephanie was, not as tender, not as sure...but a feeling for Sophia that was completely unique. And whenever the strangeness of the far-future Earth frightened Temple, whenever he felt a situation might get the better of him, whenever doubt clouded judgment, he would remember the tall lithe girl who had walked to her death that a world might have the freedom she barely had tasted. And together with Stephanie he would be able to do anything.

Unless, he thought dreamily as he drifted off to sleep, his head pillowed again on Stephanie's lap, he'd wind up with a bum jaw the rest of his life.

THE END

If you've enjoyed this book, you will not want to miss these terrific titles…

ARMCHAIR SCI-FI & HORROR DOUBLE NOVELS, $12.95 each

D-1   **THE GALAXY RAIDERS** by William P. McGivern
       SPACE STATION #1 by Frank Belknap Long

D-2   **THE PROGRAMMED PEOPLE** by Jack Sharkey
       SLAVES OF THE CRYSTAL BRAIN by William Carter Sawtelle

D-3   **YOU'RE ALL ALONE** by Fritz Leiber
       THE LIQUID MAN by Bernard C. Gilford

D-4   **CITADEL OF THE STAR LORDS** by Edmund Hamilton
       VOYAGE TO ETERNITY by Milton Lesser

D-5   **IRON MEN OF VENUS** by Don Wilcox
       THE MAN WITH ABSOLUTE MOTION by Noel Loomis

D-6   **WHO SOWS THE WIND…** by Rog Phillips
       THE PUZZLE PLANET by Robert A. W. Lowndes

D-7   **PLANET OF DREAD** by Murray Leinster
       TWICE UPON A TIME by Charles L. Fontenay

D-8   **THE TERROR OUT OF SPACE** by Dwight V. Swain
       QUEST OF THE GOLDEN APE by Ivar Jorgensen and Adam Chase

D-9   **SECRET OF MARRACOTT DEEP** by Henry Slesar
       PAWN OF THE BLACK FLEET by Mark Clifton.

D-10   **BEYOND THE RINGS OF SATURN** by Robert Moore Williams
       A MAN OBSESSED by Alan E. Nourse

ARMCHAIR SCIENCE FICTION CLASSICS, $12.95 each

C-1   **THE GREEN MAN**
       by Harold M. Sherman

C-2   **A TRACE OF MEMORY**
       By Keith Laumer

C-3   **INTO PLUTONIAN DEPTHS**
       by Stanton A. Coblentz

ARMCHAIR MASTERS OF SCIENCE FICTION SERIES, $16.95 each

M-1   **MASTERS OF SCIENCE FICTION, Vol. One**
       Bryce Walton—"Dark of the Moon" and other tales

M-2   **MASTERS OF SCIENCE FICTION, Vol. Two**
       Jerome Bixby—"One Way Street" and other tales

If you've enjoyed this book, you will not want to miss these terrific titles…

ARMCHAIR SCI-FI & HORROR DOUBLE NOVELS, $12.95 each

D-11 **PERIL OF THE STARMEN** by Kris Neville
THE STRANGE INVASION by Murray Leinster

D-12 **THE STAR LORD** by Boyd Ellanby
CAPTIVES OF THE FLAME by Samuel R. Delany

D-13 **MEN OF THE MORNING STAR** by Edmund Hamilton
PLANET FOR PLUNDER by Hal Clement and Sam Merwin, Jr.

D-14 **ICE CITY OF THE GORGON** by Chester S. Geier and Richard Shaver
WHEN THE WORLD TOTTERED by Lester del Rey

D-15 **WORLDS WITHOUT END** by Clifford D. Simak
THE LAVENDER VINE OF DEATH by Don Wilcox

D-16 **SHADOW ON THE MOON** by Joe Gibson
ARMAGEDDON EARTH by Geoff St. Reynard

D-17 **THE GIRL WHO LOVED DEATH** by Paul W. Fairman
SLAVE PLANET by Laurence M. Janifer

D-18 **SECOND CHANCE** by J. F. Bone
MISSION TO A DISTANT STAR by Frank Belknap Long

D-19 **THE SYNDIC** by C. M. Kornbluth
FLIGHT TO FOREVER by Poul Anderson

D-20 **SOMEWHERE I'LL FIND YOU** by Milton Lesser
THE TIME ARMADA by Fox B. Holden

ARMCHAIR SCIENCE FICTION CLASSICS, $12.95 each

C-4 **CORPUS EARTHLING**
by Louis Charbonneau

C-5 **THE TIME DISSOLVER**
by Jerry Sohl

C-6 **WEST OF THE SUN**
by Edgar Pangborn

ARMCHAIR SCI-FI & HORROR GEMS SERIES, $12.95 each

G-1 **SCIENCE FICTION GEMS, Vol. One**
Isaac Asimov and others

G-2 **HORROR GEMS, Vol. One**
Carl Jacobi and others

If you've enjoyed this book, you will not want to miss these terrific titles...

ARMCHAIR SCI-FI & HORROR DOUBLE NOVELS, $12.95 each

D-21   **EMPIRE OF EVIL** by Robert Arnette
      THE SIGN OF THE TIGER by Alan E. Nourse & J. A. Meyer

D-22   **OPERATION SQUARE PEG** by Frank Belknap Long
      ENCHANTRESS OF VENUS by Leigh Brackett

D-23   **THE LIFE WATCH** by Lester del Rey
      CREATURES OF THE ABYSS by Murray Leinster

D-24   **LEGION OF LAZARUS** by Edmond Hamilton
      STAR HUNTER by Andre Norton

D-25   **EMPIRE OF WOMEN** by John Fletcher
      ONE OF OUR CITIES IS MISSING by Irving Cox

D-26   **THE WRONG SIDE OF PARADISE** by Raymond F. Jones
      THE INVOLUNTARY IMMORTALS by Rog Phillips

D-27   **EARTH QUARTER** by Damon Knight
      ENVOY TO NEW WORLDS by Keith Laumer

D-28   **SLAVES TO THE METAL HORDE** by Milton Lesser
      HUNTERS OUT OF TIME by Joseph E. Kelleam

D-29   **RX JUPITER SAVE US** by Ward Moore
      BEWARE THE USURPERS by Geoff St. Reynard

D-30   **SECRET OF THE SERPENT** by Don Wilcox
      CRUSADE ACROSS THE VOID by Dwight V. Swain

ARMCHAIR SCIENCE FICTION CLASSICS, $12.95 each

C-7   **THE SHAVER MYSTERY, Book One**
      by Richard S. Shaver

C-8   **THE SHAVER MYSTERY, Book Two**
      by Richard S. Shaver

C-9   **MURDER IN SPACE**
      by David V. Reed

ARMCHAIR MASTERS OF SCIENCE FICTION SERIES, $16.95 each

M-3   **MASTERS OF SCIENCE FICTION, Vol. Three**
      Robert Sheckley, "The Perfect Woman" and other tales

M-4   **MASTERS OF SCIENCE FICTION, Vol. Four**
      Mack Reynolds, Part One, "Stowaway" and other tales

If you've enjoyed this book, you will not want to miss these terrific titles…

ARMCHAIR SCI-FI & HORROR DOUBLE NOVELS, $12.95 each

D-31   **A HOAX IN TIME** by Keith Laumer
INSIDE EARTH by Poul Anderson

D-32   **TERROR STATION** by Dwight V. Swain
THE WEAPON FROM ETERNITY by Dwight V. Swain

D-33   **THE SHIP FROM INFINITY** by Edmond Hamilton
TAKEOFF by C. M. Kornbluth

D-34   **THE METAL DOOM** by David H. Keller
TWELVE TIMES ZERO by Howard Browne

D-35   **HUNTERS OUT OF SPACE** by Joseph Kelleam
INVASION FROM THE DEEP by Paul W. Fairman,

D-36   **THE BEES OF DEATH** by Robert Moore Williams
A PLAGUE OF PYTHONS by Frederik Pohl

D-37   **THE LORDS OF QUARMALL** by Fritz Leiber and Harry Fischer
BEACON TO ELSEWHERE by James H. Schmitz

D-38   **BEYOND PLUTO** by John S. Campbell
ARTERY OF FIRE by Thomas N. Scortia

D-39   **SPECIAL DELIVERY** by Kris Neville
NO TIME FOR TOFFEE by Charles F. Meyers

D-40   **RECALLED TO LIFE** by Robert Silverberg
JUNGLE IN THE SKY by Milton Lesser

ARMCHAIR SCIENCE FICTION CLASSICS, $12.95 each

C-10   **MARS IS MY DESTINATION**
by Frank Belknap Long

C-11   **SPACE PLAGUE**
by George O. Smith

C-12   **SO SHALL YE REAP**
by Rog Phillips

ARMCHAIR SCI-FI & HORROR GEMS SERIES, $12.95 each

G-3   **SCIENCE FICTION GEMS, Vol. Two**
James Blish and others

G-4   **HORROR GEMS, Vol. Two**
Joseph Payne Brennan and others